THE JUNIPER COURT SERIES

T H E
Knock

EMME BURTON

Printed in the United States of America
First Printing, 2018

Emme Burton Books, LLC
St. Louis, MO 63122
www.emmeburton.com

Edited by Janine Savage, Write Divas, LLC
Formatting by Jason Anderson, Polgarus Studio
Cover by Teresa Conner of Wolfsparrow Publishing

Dedicated to my amazing fellow authors of Juniper Court: Isabelle, Phoebe, Sylvie, Lainie, Jennifer, and Vicki.

And to my Mom, Beth. The O.G. Cougar

The Knock Playlist

Who Knew-P!nk
Whole Lotta Love-Led Zeppelin
Castle on the Hill-Ed Sheeran
Perfect-Ed Sheeran
Breakdown-Tom Petty and The Heartbreakers
Our House-Crosby, Stills and Nash
Today My Life Begins-Bruno Mars
Foo Fighters-Everlong

Introduction

Welcome to Juniper Court.

In the summer of 2017, Isabelle Peterson came up with this kooky idea to have a series of books with each house having its own very different story. The characters would have shared scenes, giving readers glimpses into the lives of the various neighbors. She could have written the whole series on her own, but she was looking for more. She wanted a variety of flavors in the neighborhood. What better way to do that than have different authors 'adopt' a house on the block!

So, she got busy digging into her connections and considered her various author friends strengths. She had Indie Author friends who write such diverse topics and with different styles, the scope of the project, Juniper Court, more dynamic and exciting. You'll encounter authors who specialize in various sub-genre within the Romance World.

Over the past several months, the authors of Juniper court have come together, each in charge of her own home on this quiet suburban cul-de-sac where everyone seems to have secrets.

There are several things about this series that make it unique. Each book on Juniper Court can stand alone. They don't have to be read in order.

As you read, you'll see interactions with neighbors, and some of those interactions you'll find in other books, from the other perspective. Enjoy these glimpses behind the doors of the neighbors and then, click on their books and get the full story.

From Sweet to Swingers…
from LGBT to BDSM…
It's happening behind the doors of
—Juniper Court.

Learn more about all the books and the authors on our website:
www.junipercourtseries.com

"I'm not afraid of you running away, baby.
I get the feeling you won't."
"Breakdown," Tom Petty

Chapter 1

I'm in my usual morning spot in the dining room, curled up with a cup of coffee between my hands in the sole club chair that Donnie bought me. I'm looking out the bay window of the house that Donnie bought me and over the large yard that Donnie bought me.

Donovan Garrett didn't select the chair or the house or pick out the landscaping in the yard. He couldn't. He was gone, but the money he left behind, or rather the insurance policy and settlement from the wrongful death lawsuit, paid for all of it.

Donovan was my husband. He was also a police detective. An undercover one. In vice. He lived through countless embeds and two bullet wounds—once, very gravely, in the upper left shoulder near his heart while undercover in a stalker-near-kidnapping case, a few years ago.

He was never supposed to buy me a house on Juniper Court in the warm, idyllic town of Sunview. No, we were supposed to raise our kids and grow old together in St. Louis. Live through each blazing humid summer and frigid ice-storm-ridden winter together.

I wasn't supposed to be here alone.

I'd always known the day could come, but on that day, "the knock" on the door took me by surprise.

Donnie was supposed to be home soon. I knew he had just completed his last ever undercover assignment. He was moving on to an administrative desk job and I was thrilled. I wouldn't have to worry anymore about where he was for weeks at a time. I wouldn't have to hear information through a secure line to the police department. I would have him at my dinner table and in my bed every night. We had survived ten years of danger and probably more peril than Donnie was allowed to divulge to me, and now it would be our time. Our time to enjoy our now ten- and eight-year-old sons, Donovan "Van" Jr. and Shane.

I never got my nightly family dinners or my nightly kiss good-night.

I never got my husband back from his undercover life. Not because of a bullet or a knife—but because of an accident.

Knock, knock!

Why in the world would Donovan knock? Did he forget his key? I don't even think I locked the door because I told him I'd wait up for him after his text half an hour ago.

> POSEY, BABE, I'm done. It's over. I'm out forever. The arrests are happening right now. Tomorrow starts a whole new life.

He would never know how prophetic his words were.

I padded to the door, sleepy-headed and confused, after dozing off while I waited for Donnie.

I opened the door, expecting the love of my life, but it wasn't Donnie. It was one of his fellow detectives, Aaron, in street clothes, flanked by a couple of uniformed officers. My heart fell.

"Hello, Posey." Aaron's voice was stiff and formal.

"Aaron?" I moved side to side, peering behind him to find Donnie. Where was Donnie? This had happened before—officers at my door—when Donnie had been shot.

"Posey." Aaron's head dropped, and he sniffed and swallowed. I grabbed the doorframe. This was not good. Not good at all. Aaron lifted his head and pinned me in his gaze. His eyes were rimmed red and filled with tears.

"NO!" I tried to scream, but it came out as a choked, dysphonic plea.

Aaron stepped toward me and wrapped an arm around me to keep me from falling.

"Let's go inside. Off the porch. We need privacy."

Somehow, I found myself sitting on the couch. An officer on either side of me, with an arm around me. Aaron sat on the coffee table in front of me, holding both my hands.

"Posey, Donovan is dead."

The words ricocheted around the room, and in my head, and finally slammed into my chest and I gasped for air.

The only word I seemed to be able to form was NO. Over and over in my consciousness and on my lips.

Aaron gave me a bit of time but then gently brought me back. "Posey, listen to me, look at me."

I found his eyes, which held all the pain I was feeling.

A wet film formed over my own eyes and blurred my vision.

"Donovan finished the assignment. He was on his way to the

station to change and debrief. A drunk driver came into his lane and forced him into the guardrail. Posey, Donnie's car flipped over the guardrail and impacted in the ravine below. It became engulfed in flames before anyone could reach him."

Every cell in my body felt like it was screaming and shaking, but I was stock-still. Unable to move, breathe, focus. My lips and nose started to tingle. I turned my face away from Aaron and the room spun. Then I stood and ran.

To the kitchen.

To the sink.

Where I vomited, while gripping the thick edge of the farm sink. That was right before my legs crumpled beneath me. I felt an excruciating pain on my cheek as I went down. I felt like I was dying. I wished I had died.

When I came to, Aaron and the other guys' faces were above me. I reached up and felt something hot and sticky on my face and could taste metal in my mouth. I moved to stand up.

"No, Posey, stay down. You slammed your face on the sink when you fainted."

"I fainted?"

"Yes, you ran in here and vomited in the sink."

I remembered that part.

"And then you collapsed and connected pretty hard on the way down."

That I did not remember.

"Mom!" A cracking preteen voice stops my journey through that painful memory.

"Momma?"

I shake myself out of the past and look up from my coffee

cup. My boys—my loves—Van and Shane stand in front of me with puzzled looks on their faces.

"Hi! Hi, guys!" I stand up, set my coffee cup on the end table, place an arm around each of their shoulders and bring them in for a group hug. I hold on a little too long.

Shane squirms out of my embrace. "Mooom!"

"OK, OK." I let them both loose.

They move toward the front door. "Did you eat breakfast?" I ask, my parenting mode finally kicking in.

Backs to me, they both hold up Nutri-Grain bars as they leave the house. The door slams loudly behind them. It no sooner crashes against the doorjamb than it opens again and Van's head peers around. "Mom, don't forget, that guy is coming tonight."

What guy? "What guy?" my lips mimic my thought.

"That guitar guy. The one you called for me? He's coming over for my first lesson after school."

"Oh, that's right. Yeah. Thanks for reminding me."

I barely recognize myself. Who is this laissez-faire parent? This barely attentive, lost in her own grief person? Mornings are bad. Nights are worse. Even though I spent many, many days without Donnie when he was undercover, it's just knowing I won't ever see him or hear him again that makes it so excruciating. Some days I go a few hours without thinking of him. When I do, I admonish myself for letting his memory slip away.

Grief reminds me of a crazy, sad amusement park ride. You never know when a turn or spin will come that makes you sick to your stomach and wrenches tears from your eyes.

Oh, and there's no way to get off the ride.

If I have a faraway look at times, it's because I'm imagining how soft his hair felt when I bent down to kiss it, the last time I saw him.

Someday, I'll stop counting the days since he left, but not yet.

Chapter 2

Since it's Tuesday, I work from home. Tuesdays and Thursdays are my days to get my designs done. The opposite days, office days, are filled with meetings and lunches and sometimes too much "people time." But every other day I get up, have my giant cup of coffee, throw on a T-shirt, my favorite cutoff sweats and work in my bare feet. When I started at Two-Shot Graphics, I set it up so I could work from home part of the time. I don't need to work, I want to, and Two-Shot works perfectly.

My design space is a quiet retreat. I can come in here, shut the door and create. Currently, Two-Shot is responsible for the graphics on a large campaign for the album and tour of the hugely popular group, #coolNerd, fronted by songwriter-guitarist Sid Cooper. If my boys knew, they would freak. He's one of their favorite artists. There's a possibility of seeing him in concert when he comes to town. I won't tell them until the job is over because I'd hate to disappoint them if it didn't pan out. I hate to disappoint anyone. I hate to do anything wrong, even if unintentional.

It's that very quality that led me to Donovan.

"Oh my God, we narrowly avoided that ticket." The police car pulled over the car behind me even though I clearly ran the red light, too.

I turned to the passenger seated next to me. "I'm going back."

"Argh, Posey, you can't go back. Besides, the cop is busy." Drew, my boyfriend at the time, moaned loudly.

"Well, I'm just gonna… I'm just gonna stop and call the police department."

"Really, Posey, most people run away from getting a ticket."

"But, Drew, I need to do the right thing, and I clearly ran that light."

"Whatever." Drew huffed and started frantically swiping at the screen on his phone.

I pulled into a parking lot and called the City of St. Louis Police Department. I explained that I ran a red light at Kingshighway and Manchester and I wanted to tell the police officer I was sorry.

"Uh, uhm… really? Like, who does that?" the dispatcher stuttered.

"Me, I guess. I don't like the feeling of being… wrong."

"OK, one moment." The phone went quiet before it clicked over.

"Hello? Hello?" I squeaked into the phone. "This is Posey…"

"This is Officer Garrett. How can I help you?" The dispatcher put me through to the actual police officer.

"Hi, I'm so sorry. We ran a red light at Kingshighway and Manchester, and… uhm… we'll come back and pay, get the ticket. My name is Posey—"

"Spence," the officer interjected.

"Yes, that's right, Posey Spence. How did you know?"

"I ran your plates after you ran the red light."

"Well, we'll come back and pay because you snagged the guy behind us and not us."

"Yeah, I had to choose between the two of you and he was closer. He ran it after you did, so he's slightly guiltier. Don't worry, he's one of the hockey players for the Blues. He can afford the fine. Hell, his attorney will probably get the ticket thrown out. Just wondering why you keep saying 'we' and 'us'?"

"There's another person in the car with me."

"Don't involve me in this," Drew complained loudly.

"Your boyfriend?" the officer asked.

I liked his deep, scratchy voice. I liked that he was curious about who I was with.

"Sorta," I whispered. I didn't know why I whispered. Drew wasn't paying attention to me.

"Listen, Posey. We'll let it go. Next time you're in this part of town, drive more carefully."

"Where are you?" I blurted out, thoughtlessly. I had an overwhelming desire to meet this polite, pardoning, rough-voiced man.

"What?"

"Where are you? I want to meet you. To thank you."

"But you're—"

"Yeah, I'm… in the parking lot of the donut shop by the intersection where I ran the light." It was my turn to cut him off.

"For someone who ran a light, you didn't get very far."

"I felt bad."

"Funny, most people feel victorious after getting out of a ticket."

"Not me. I'm… different."

"Clearly."

"I'm a rule follower."

"Posey?"

"Yes?"

"I'm parked next to you."

I turned. There was a police cruiser right next to me. The officer in it was on the phone and he waved at me. He was a handsome ginger.

"Hi," I said on the phone as I waved back in person.

"Why don't you get out of your car and meet me by mine."

"OK."

I hung up and looked at Drew. "I'll be right back."

He threw his hands in the air. "Jesus, Pose. Really?"

"Yes, really. He was nice. I should thank him." I checked my makeup and hair in the mirror before I hopped out of the car.

When I rounded the back of the cruiser, Officer Garrett was already out of his vehicle, standing with one hand on the door handle. For some reason, I was stopped in my tracks by his presence. He was tall, broad-chested with a strong jaw. He stepped forward until he was about a foot away from me.

"Hello, Posey," He pulled off his mirrored aviators, slipped one of the earpieces into a hole in his shirt and locked me with his gaze. Then he took out his ticket book. "Can you confirm your address and phone number?"

I told him both automatically.

"So, you're giving me a ticket?" I asked, a strange panicky

sound infusing my voice.

"No, a verbal warning." He took the ticket and put it in his breast pocket.

I released the breath I didn't even know I was holding with a big sigh. "Thank you."

He patted his breast pocket. "I'd like to call you, if that's OK. I like that whole 'rule follower' thing."

He wanted to call me? Yes, please! I nodded my head eagerly and he grinned. A huge, genuine grin.

When he handed me his card, his finger grazed mine. A flash of excitement moved through me. I read the card—Officer Donovan Garrett. City of St. Louis Police—and then I turned to go.

"You drive carefully, Posey. No more risk-taking."

"Yes, Officer Garrett." I looked at the card and then corrected myself, "Yes, Donovan."

I love our origin story. Nobody ever believes I picked up *him* after a traffic violation. Donovan had said he knew I was special the minute I said I'd wanted to do the right thing. Maybe even loved me.

My cell phone chirps. Something or someone is always dragging me back from my memories. It's a good thing, too. If they didn't I'd probably live there. It's where I'm happiest. And for that I feel terrible for my children, but it's true.

The text is from my boss, Beckham. He's just checking my progress. The initial artwork for #coolNerd is due Friday. I assure him it will be done. I haven't even started.

Chapter 3

I've been listening to #coolNerd's newest album. I've listened at least seven times, and I think I've finally hit upon something. The whole thing is about leaving home, finding yourself, or thinking you've found yourself but not until you find the person who makes it all make sense. The lyrics are so layered and real. I decide to do more research about Sid Cooper and #coolNerd.

The front door slams, signaling that the kids are home from school.

"We're here!" they yell.

"K! Did you have a good day?"

"Yeah."

I plug in my earbuds because #coolNerd's album isn't released yet, and I'm under strict orders not to share or leak or even mention it. Which is too bad because it's really good, and I'd love to talk about it with someone.

As the last song on the album plays out, I look at my watch. Shit! It's five o'clock! I need to get dinner started. I pull the buds from my ears.

Knock! Knock!

Who's knocking on the front door? I mean we have a doorbell for God's sake. Knocking is for emergencies only. Something urgent. Something bad. Don't people know that?

I pad to the front door, my bare feet smacking against the tiles in the entryway. I swear to God if this is a salesman or a kid selling cookies, I'm gonna freak!

I open the door about to admonish the said "knocker," but instead I'm met with a pair of deep green eyes crinkled up by a sheepish grin that spreads into a huge smile.

"Hi!" The voice attached to the green eyes says through the screen door. "I'm Mitch Morgan." The green eyes look me up and down, and for some reason it doesn't bother me. Mitch is carrying a guitar case over one shoulder.

"Is Mrs. Garrett here?"

I push the screen door open. "I'm Mrs. Garrett."

"No," he corrects me, disbelief in his voice. His eyes sweep over me again, this time stopping at my feet, then my Led Zeppelin T-shirt and finally my face. "I mean, are you sure? Because you don't look like a mom… oh, crap… uh… I better shut up!"

I laugh aloud and ask, "Was that an awkwardly charming left-handed compliment?"

"If you're willing to take it that way, then, yes. Yes, it was."

"I will."

"Good. Like I said, I'm Mitch Morgan. I'm here for Van's guitar lesson."

This guy is my kid's guitar teacher? Holy smokes, he's

adorable. I mean, objectively, no one can deny how good-looking this guy is. Tall, short brown hair, scruffy beard and a jawline that could cut glass.

"M-Mitch. Yes. Guitar. Yes. Yes. Come in. Please," I stutter after I've finished ogling him. My stomach flips as I step back to let him into the foyer. I push a lock of hair behind my ear and become very aware that I'm dressed like a complete slob and my hair is in the messiest messy bun known to exist on this planet or any other. I can't even remember if I put on makeup today.

"Excuse me." I hold up a finger and then walk away from the much-too-handsome musician occupying all the space and air and everything else in my foyer. Seriously, I need to take a breath. I knock on Van's door and immediately open it.

"Hey, Kiddo. Van. Come out here. There's someone I want you to meet."

Van throws his tablet down and jumps off his bed. "Is it the guitar teacher?"

"Yep. I forgot he was coming. Come out and meet him."

Van joins me in the hall and we walk down the hallway.

"Mom, I reminded you this morning."

"I know. I was focused on work when he knocked on the door."

Mr. Green Eyes watches us come down the hall. He shifts the papers from his right hand to under his left arm and reaches out to shake Van's hand.

They shake with one of those "cool guy swing-your-arm-out-then- shake-with-your-hands-over-each-other grip" handshakes. The kind that are generally followed by a bro hug, but it's probably too soon for that.

"Hey, man! Nice to meet you. I'm Mitch."

"I'm Van."

I interrupt, "Mitch, I'm so glad my boss asked your friend about guitar teachers. I don't know if I'd have found one with such high recommendations without him."

"Yeah, my friend's a good guy. Don't see him enough. I'm happy he thought of me for this job." Mitch's voice is warm and sincere. His eyes never break from mine when he talks to me.

I turn to Van. "Why don't you grab your guitar and go up to the bonus room for your lesson. I set up a corner for you as a rehearsal space. I'll get dinner started so it's ready when you're done."

Van nods and signals Mitch to follow him. As they walk away, Mitch asks Van who his favorite artist is and what he likes to play.

The only part I can make out is the word "#coolNerd".

Chapter 4

Once Van and Mitch's voices fade, I scurry to my bedroom and straight through to the bathroom. Facing the mirror, I already know what I'll see before I do. One glance confirms it. Traces of makeup from the day before grace my eyes along with the huge dark circles under them. I look like an exhausted raccoon. My usually sideswept bangs are weirdly parted in the middle and askew from my habit of running my hand through them as I work. My messy bun is a matted disaster cocked somewhere between the ten forty-five and eleven o'clock positions on top of my head. I don't even bother to look at my T-shirt and cutoffs. I know they're probably horrifying, but they're clean. The least I can do is clean up my hair and face. After all, we have company. Very handsome company.

Part of me is shocked I care at all.

The other part is pleased that I do.

I mechanically clean my face, slick on some concealer and mascara and a swipe of lip gloss. That's better. To put in any more effort would be weird, right? I mean, he's a guitar teacher, not a date. A date? Why am I even thinking these things?

I rake the ponytail holder out of my hair, tame my bangs to the side and comb my tangled blond hair. Then I smooth it into a ponytail high on the back of my head. Again, better. Maybe I should change clothes?

"Mom!" yells Shane from the doorway to my bathroom. "Are we gonna eat soon? I'm getting hungry." He's my sweet, brown-eyed ten-year-old, whose smile is a copy of his father's.

No time to change clothes. I look in the mirror one more time. What am I even doing? When's the last time I cared this much about the way I looked? I know. The last time I said goodbye to Donnie.

"Yeah, baby, I was just combing my hair. It was crazy." After taking one last stab at controlling my bangs, I turn to him. "Let's go make dinner and we'll eat when Van is done with guitar lessons."

"Great! I can hear them. I think that guitar teacher is really good. I can hear him playing songs and they sound just like they do on my iPhone."

"Really? Let's go sneak a listen." Shane and I creep down the hall and listen at the bottom of the stairs to the bonus room.

Shane's right. Mitch is good. He's playing a Jimmy Page riff, I think.

I whisper to my youngest, "Come on, let's let them play and go make dinner. It's Tuesday, so that means it's…"

"Tacos!"

"You got it, buddy."

In the kitchen, Shane and I turn the radio on to the local classic-rock station. I have to give Donnie the credit for my kids' love of real rock music. They might be the only eighth and fifth graders with the ability to sing Beatles songs by heart.

I brown the ground beef and add taco seasoning as Shane chops some lettuce and tomatoes, and gets out the shredded cheese, salsa and sour cream. Our little family of three has this down pat. We can put together a meal in no time because we eat the same five meals during the week. So far, nobody has complained. Maybe it's because they know it's all I can handle. Funny, I've never thought about or questioned it until now. Never even thought to ask the boys if it bothered them. It's been a strange night. Things that I've taken for granted are really coming to light.

Like my appearance and what I'm doing or not doing for my kids.

Dinner is set up at the kitchen island. We'd stopped being a "dinner table family" during the times when Donnie was undercover. It didn't feel right to sit at the dinner table with him not there. Then when he would never be there again, we stopped eating at it altogether. We didn't have a meeting to discuss not eating at the table. We just fell into sitting in the tall stools facing the kitchen. We have a dinner table—only now it's usually covered in bills and school papers.

Laughter echoes down the hall. A deep, rich man's voice and a squeaky preteen's.

"Man, you've got some chops, Mitch."

"Chops? Who told you the word chops? That's like an old musician's word."

"My dad."

My heart lifts and sinks in quick succession. *My dad.* The words are heaven and hell when said aloud.

"Your dad's a smart guy," Mitch says kindly.

"Was," Van informs Mitch matter-of-factly.

"What?" Shock fills Mitch's response.

"Was. He's dead."

"Oh, man. Van, I am so sorry, dude."

"It's OK."

"Yeah?"

"It's OK, we have Mom. As long as Mom's OK, we're OK."

Wow, I didn't know he felt that way.

"Then you're good, because your Mom seems OK," Mitch says as they both enter the kitchen.

Our eyes connect. I smile to let him know I heard the compliment.

"Wow, it smells great in here, Mom."

"It sure does," Mitch agrees, returning my smile.

"Hey, Mom, can Mitch stay for dinner?"

I hadn't thought of that possibility, but I'm not opposed. "Well, uh…"

"Come on, Mom!" Van implores.

Shane simultaneously says, "Yeah, we never have company except Grandma and Grandpa."

There's a frantic overlapping of invitation and polite refusal and finally it's agreed that Mitch will stay for Taco Tuesday.

"Shane, can you get another plate?" Shane is out of his seat and grabbing all the needed dinnerware before I've even finished the question.

"I hope you don't mind sitting at the island."

Mitch smiles as he slides onto the barstool between Van and Shane. "I just think it's cool you all still eat together. Really, I don't think it matters what or where or how you eat together. Just that you do."

Van whispers to Shane, "That sounds like Dad."

I'm sure he thinks I didn't hear him, but I did.

The boys are more animated than I've seen them in a long time, or maybe I just haven't noticed for a long time. Dinner is filled with stories of guitars and songs Mitch likes and tales from school. When we're all finished, the boys clear the plates. Mitch offers to help with the dishes, but I don't feel right making him clean up since he only bargained on teaching guitar, not staying for dinner, too.

"Well, I have to get going, Van, Shane, Mrs. Garrett." Mitch picks up his guitar case from a nearby chair and slings it over his shoulder.

"Mitch, please call me Posey."

"OK, not gonna argue with that." Mitch holds both hands up in mock surrender. He lowers his hand, places one on his flat stomach and one behind his back and bows slightly. "Thank you for dinner, Posey." The move is goofy. And adorable. And makes me smile.

The boys say their goodbyes and run down the hall to Van's room. I walk Mitch to the door.

"You know, Van has great potential. You might want to think about more frequent lessons."

"Really?" I stop.

Mitch turns back to me and laughs, one deep chuckle. "Yes, really. I'm not saying this just to get more work. He seems to have his basics down."

"His dad taught him."

Mitch clears his throat. "I'm so sorry about your husband. You should know he did a good job teaching Van. Sounds like a good guy."

There is a hitch in my voice when I say, "Thank you." I clear it and ask, "So, could you come twice a week? Like maybe Thursdays, too?"

"Let me give you a call tomorrow. I think Thursdays could work." Mitch smiles and the edges of his eyes crinkle up, just the way they did when I answered the door. It looks familiar and I recall Donnie's crinkled up the same way.

Mitch extends his hand and I take it. A sparking, charged sensation moves through my palm and straight up my arm and across my breasts. He looks me in the eyes the entire time. I'm engulfed by the greenness of his eyes.

In a warm tone he says, "Bye, Posey."

I don't know when he let go of my hand, because I'm too concerned with why I'm not breathing and when I will start again. Something about his touch excites and alarms me all at once. So much so that I immediately anticipate the next time we'll talk.

Tomorrow! He said he'd call tomorrow.

Chapter 5

I've been so distracted in my morning meetings at Two-Shot today. I had to ask people to repeat themselves no less than four times. My mind keeps replaying my time with Mitch—frame by frame, like a movie—while I wait for his phone call.

Absentmindedly, I run my fingers through my hair, only to get them stuck in the dried-out split ends. That's it! I'm taking an extra-long lunch. I need a haircut. I look at my unpainted nails and ragged cuticles. I need a manicure, too. Maybe an entire makeover. It's been ages since I've given a thought about my appearance or spent a dime on anything just for me, but for some reason I do now. I feel a little silly that the tiny morsel of attention some handsome young guy gave me has me feeling so self-conscious, but when I looked in the mirror last night, I barely recognized the frumpy woman staring back. I gaze down at my hands. Donnie always liked when I had my nails done. I guess with him not around, it didn't seem important anymore. It is important! I like having nice nails and hair, too. Extra-long lunch it is!

After grabbing my bag and laptop, I dash across the room to a glassed-in office space and tap on the glass. Beckham looks up. I slide open the door a few inches and poke my head in. "Boss, I'm going out for lunch."

"Uh, OK." Beckham appears to be off-balance.

Is this so unusual for me? I make a snap decision.

"Aaaand after lunch, I'm going home. I have a great idea for the #coolNerd graphics." I really don't, but Beckham won't see any of it until I'm ready to show him, so it's fine.

"Great!" Beckham gives me a thumbs-up. I guess sliding the part in about working made the whole "not coming back to the office" thing OK. I've never really done anything like this before. Generally, it would fall into the category of "wrong" for me. Not precisely the rules. But really it isn't. I'm salaried. As long as I get my work done, it doesn't matter where or when I do it. And how many times have I pulled an all-nighter to get artwork ready for a pitch or presentation? Good Lord, I need to stop arguing and rationalizing with myself so much.

Once I get in my car, I text Valley, my neighbor. One of the only neighbors I have a phone number for.

> ME: Hey, Do you know where I can get a haircut and color last minute? I know I'm asking for a miracle.

A text comes back immediately.

> VALLEY: Really???? I've been dying for you to get your hair done!

She has?

ME: You have? Why didn't you say something?

VALLEY: Hair is very personal. And it hasn't seemed like the right time to bring it up. Yet. Did something happen to make you want a makeover?

ME: Nothing specific.

Liar.

ME: Just time for an update. We'll talk about it tonight when I pick up Shane.

VALLEY: OK, give me a few minutes to see what I can do. Anytime this afternoon OK?

ME: Yes

I stop texting, place my phone on the console between the seats and pull away from the Two-Shot parking lot. I might as well grab something at Panini, the sandwich shop around the corner.

What I'm doing this afternoon? Waiting for phone calls. From Valley about a hair appointment. From Mitch about adding lessons for Van on Thursday. I check my phone to make sure my ringer is on. I wouldn't want to miss either one. I don't know which one I'm more anxious to receive. Who am I kidding? The one from Mitch.

I make my way into Panini and order a chicken Cobb salad with green goddess dressing. It's not very crowded since the lunch rush is over. My name is called before I finish filling my plastic cup with iced coffee. I pick up my meal from the counter, find a seat and pull my phone out and place it on the table. Why won't this thing ring?

I make it three quarters of the way through my meal when my phone whistles that a text message has arrived.

> VALLEY: Girl, I used my magical powers and got you into Francisco Marco Salon at 1:45. You have 15 minutes to get your ass there!

Jesus, Francisco Marco! That place is exclusive. And expensive.

After sending her my thanks and a promise of many, many drinks, I toss the remainder of my salad in the trash can. On the way to my car, I take a few sips of coffee while simultaneously figuring out the navigation to Francisco Marco on my phone.

Arriving at Francisco's bang at exactly 1:44, I'm greeted at the door to the salon by none other than Francisco himself. He's about fifty-five years old, completely bald but with a fabulously groomed hipster beard. He also has beautiful blue eyes fringed with eyelashes that would make Bambi jealous.

"Are you Posey?"

"Yes."

"Ahh, you *are* the beautiful flower Valley said you were! In serious need of a bit of pruning and care, but still, *bella*!"

Can't argue that. I have split ends four inches long. I know because I inspected them thoroughly during my morning meetings. Hence my inattentiveness.

Francisco seats me at his station, drapes me carefully and begins asking questions. Not about how I'd like my hair to look, but about my life.

What do I like?

Clean lines and a modern look.

What do I do for a living?

Graphic artist, primarily for music and the arts.

Do I have kids? Yes, two very busy boys.

The entire time he's inspecting my hair, root to tip.

"Posey, when is the last time you had your hair cut?"

I bow my head and take a deep breath before answering, "Like a real haircut? At a salon?"

I look up at Francisco's reflection in the salon mirror. He nods.

"Over two years ago, but I've been trimming my bangs now and then. And I cut a bit off the ends one time." I screw up my expression and shake my head to indicate the big mistake that was. "Just one time," I say, holding up my index finger for emphasis.

Francisco shakes his head slowly and smirks. "Tsk, tsk, tsk… darling, no more. You have gorgeous hair. Don't cut it yourself again. Promise me."

I sheepishly comply. "I promise."

"From what you have said and the condition of your hair, I need to cut off quite a bit. Is that OK with you?"

"Francisco, you do what you have to do. I'm sure I'll love it. I'm way past needing a change. I think I need many changes."

"Are you telling me I have a blank canvas? Free reign? I can do whatever I like? Color?"

"Except for pink or blue hair, I'm up for anything."

"I like your hair color, but I think we could brighten it up. Make you a sparkling blonde, like you were as a kid."

After a huge exhalation, I say, "Go for it."

Two hours later, Francisco spins the chair around.

I'm blown away. It's been reimagined into a pixie with swooping long bangs that can be styled many ways. The color is also two shades lighter. "Francisco, you're a miracle worker! This is amazing." I can't stop flipping my hair around, turning my head at various angles and reaching up to touch it. There's a newfound lightness that's palpable. At least to me.

"I had a feeling your hair, and you, needed a reset."

"I didn't know it myself, but you're completely right. Thank you."

"Now, let's get your nails and makeup done."

"But, I didn't ask Valley to help with that."

"She scheduled it anyway. She must know it's much needed."

I owe Valley more than drinks.

I leave Francisco Marco Salon a different woman. At least externally. My first thought upon seeing the new me was what would Donovan think? Quickly followed by, I wonder if Mitch will notice a difference? I can't be sure, but that handshake with Mitch seems to have released something. Sensations and emotions that had been locked away for so long I thought they'd died in a tiny prison cell in my heart have been given release papers.

Chapter 6

Valley walks over as I step out of my car. She always looks like a million freaking bucks to me. So sexy in that cool, rocker chick sort of way, and her makeup is always perfect.

"Holy shit! When you said haircut, you meant haircut! It looks amazing. You look like a different person."

I run my fingers through the very short back, feeling the loss of what used to be my messy bun. "Not too much gone. Too short?"

"Hell, no, you're a smoke show. Turn around." Valley twirls her finger.

I grab my bag, shut the car door and do a twirl right in my driveway.

"And new clothes, too. I didn't even know you wore heels."

"Just new shoes and this jacket," I say, referring to the block heel sandals and long, tailored leopard-print jacket with leather trim I purchased right off the mannequin at a boutique down the street from Francisco's salon.

My phone rings. I startle and quickly fish it out of my

bag. "Mitch!" I say, thinking I only said it in my head.

"Who's Mitch?" Valley asks, her left eyebrow raised. "Other than someone who makes you jump and say his name like an orgasm."

An expression like that from Valley is not unexpected. She starts to walk away. "Answer your phone, girl. I'll send your kid home in a few."

Always obedient, I answer on the third ring, hoping I don't sound too breathless and excited.

"Uhm, hey, Posey. It's uhm, it's Mitch." He seems nervous.

"Hello, Mitch," I reply as I school my voice into a too low, phone sex operator voice. I'm a ridiculous mess. About a phone call.

"So, I moved some things around and I can start seeing Van for a second lesson each week. Is tomorrow too soon?"

"Yes, I mean no, it's not too soon. And yes, that's great!"

Why do I feel like I'm a fifteen-year-old schoolgirl whenever I talk to this guy? I haven't really noticed anyone since the moment I laid eyes on Donnie years ago, but something about Mitch feels familiar, comfortable.

Mitch laughs. Probably at my awkward response. I picture his face—his cocked smile and his crinkled eyes—and a flush comes over my body. "See you tomorrow, Posey. Same time as Tuesday's lesson. Tell Van to be ready!"

"Oh, I will. See you tomorrow."

My thoughts instantly start a countdown to five o'clock tomorrow, mentally rifling through my closet for what to wear and wondering if Mitch will like my new look.

Suddenly, I'm struck with an idea for the #coolNerd

graphics. I rush inside, pull off my new jacket and throw it and my bag onto one of the barstools at the island. I charge down the hall to my studio but peek into Van's room to tell him he has an additional lesson with Mitch each week, starting tomorrow.

"Cool," he responds.

"Oh, and I just got inspired for my latest project. I gotta get this down." I continue down the hall but yell over my shoulder, "Do you think you could throw something together for yourself and Shane for dinner? Frozen pizza, ramen, something?"

"Sure, Mom."

When I get to my office, I make a beeline for my desk, set up my laptop and turn it on. I'd planned to google Sid Cooper and never did, but now that I need some background to develop this idea, it's a good time to start. The #coolNerd album is called *You Are My New Home*, which is also the name of the first single to be released. I need to find out about Sid Cooper's home.

Sid was born in Boston, but has lived in Downers Grove, Illinois, since the age of six months when he was adopted. His mother is Kimberly Cooper, but there's little detail. I don't find a death date, so I guess she's still alive. His adoptive father's name is Gil Cooper. I wonder why his birth mother and adoptive father have the same last name. Further research reveals that Clip Cooper, former NFL player and now coach, is his brother, and Minnie Cooper Snackenberg is his sister. I think I've read some of her articles in *Vogue* or somewhere. This is a family of achievers. There's nothing about a girlfriend or wife, so I'm wondering who the "you" in "You Are My New Home" is. I shift over to images and google "Downers Grove" and am immediately captured by the photos of the town. The sweet old train station, people in a coffee shop, kids on bikes. The one that most attracts me is a photo from a time before technology kept us at home and people met in public places to talk and get information. This picture could be from the fifties or sixties, but judging by the cars and clothes it's probably more like the nineties.

Since I'm only doing a mock-up, I screenshot the picture and start on the graphics. I bookmark the page for inspiration later. If this works, we'll have to go to Chicago to get custom shots for the artwork.

I'm so involved in my work I don't hear Van and Shane knock on my studio door.

"Mom, dinner!" Shane's voice cuts through my fog of concentration as he runs into my studio.

I lift my head from the computer and turn toward the door.

Shane stops short. "Whoa! You cut your hair. Like, really short!"

My face tightens with concern. "Is it OK? Do… do you like it?" I reach up and touch the back of it.

"It's different," Van chimes in.

Shane tilts his head as he follows up with, "But cool, like Katy Perry or that girl from *Harry Potter*."

"Emma Watson," Van tells him.

"Yeah, her." Shane grins.

"OK. Katy Perry and Emma Watson are OK with me."

I'm surprised they even noticed my hair. They didn't comment on my makeup and manicure. Maybe that isn't as drastic a change. Or maybe boys don't notice things like that.

Chapter 7

I've been a wreck all day. I mean, I've been productive, kicking ass on the #coolNerd project. But I've also been singing at the top of my lungs, shaking my butt to my music turned up way too loud and randomly stopping and replaying every word Mitch has ever said to me, every look he's given me and every feeling I've had since I met him three days ago. It's preposterous that I'm this mesmerized in such short a time, but I guess stuff like this really happens.

I didn't really get a chance to greet him when he arrived for Van's Thursday lesson. Van ran to the door, sliding along the hardwood in his socks, and answered it right after the first ring.

Mitch said a hasty "Hi, Posey" as he passed by my studio door and went upstairs for Van's lesson. I scooted over to the door just in time to respond with a "Hey, Mitch" and get a peek at his very attractive ass as he ascended the stairs after Van, who was chattering like a squirrel.

Returning to my work, I realize I've been staring at the same font for ten minutes trying to make a decision, and give up. I can't concentrate hearing the rich calmness of his voice as he instructs Van. Knowing Mitch is in my house. Right above me.

It's time to make dinner anyway. Spaghetti Thursday.

The music upstairs stops and I check my watch. The lesson is over. When I look up, Van slides onto one of the stools at the kitchen island.

"Mom, Mitch is staying for dinner, OK?" Mitch enters a half second later.

"Hey, Van, buddy, what are you doing? I didn't—"

Van spins on the stool to face Mitch. "You said it smelled good and talked about how hungry you were."

Mitch's face immediately turns pink. "Yeah, but I didn't mean—"

I clear my throat. "Mitch, it's fine. I was going to invite you to stay before Van even said anything."

"Thank you. You know you don't have to feed me every time I come over."

I smile and then laugh. It feels good. To smile. To laugh without thinking about it first or forcing it. "I know, but we have plenty of spaghetti and your lessons bump up against dinnertime." I mentally add, I couldn't wait to see you and talk to you again.

Did I really say "bump up against" in a sentence?

Mitch sets his instrument and music down on the floor. "Well, thank you again." He sits on the stool next to Van and leans his chin on his hands, observing me as I brown the hamburger for the meat sauce. "Hey, I noticed when I walked by your office before that you got a haircut. It looks really great."

I look down and rub the naked back of my neck. "Thank you. I'm getting used to it." I'm probably bright pink now, too.

"It looks great on you."

I'm not used to this much attention and turn away, flustered. I walk into the hall and say, "Shane, it's almost dinnertime. Come get out the plates and silverware."

Shane groans from his room, "Just a sec, Mom. I'm about to win this race."

Mitch whispers to Van, "Must be playing Mario Kart, huh, buddy?" Then he stands up and walks into the kitchen. "Let's help your mom get the dishes out so Shane can cross the finish line."

Impressive.

He does the same after dinner. "Guys, go ahead and play your game. I'll help your mom clean up."

"Mitch—" Once again I protest.

"Posey." Mitch says in counterprotest. And without another word, we clean the kitchen. I'm struck by how smoothly we work together, clearing dishes, him rinsing, me filling the dishwasher.

I ask Mitch about his work and am not surprised to hear, like most people in their twenties, he has more than one job. Besides giving guitar lessons, he substitute teaches and does some session work for local musicians.

"What do you do, Posey? I mean I know you work from home."

"I work for Two-Shot, and I only work from home two days a week. They just happen to be the days of Van's lessons."

"The graphics company?"

"You know it?"

"Yeah, my friend uses them for some stuff. What do you do?"

"I'm a graphic artist." I bite my lip. I'm supposed to keep the #coolNerd account to myself. I signed a nondisclosure and everything, but I'm going to take a chance. "Do you want to see what I'm working on?"

"Absolutely!"

He is actually interested in my work. I have to say, Donovan was supportive but never seemed truly interested. I throw down the dish towel after wiping my hands and tilt my head toward the hall.

I'm about to open the door, but before I do, I turn back to Mitch with a very serious expression. "You cannot, under any circumstances, tell anyone I showed you this."

Mitch kisses two fingers on his right hand and crosses his heart. It's adorable.

I slowly open the door. "Come on in." Mitch is only inches behind me. I feel his breath. The little hairs on my neck and shoulders and arms stand on end.

"Wow! This is so cool!" Mitch walks around my office, looking at the framed album art and concert posters from some of the work I've done in the past. He stops, mouth agape, in front of one of the covers with a platinum record framed alongside it. "Is this Boxwood?"

"Yep." I stand next to Mitch, our upper arms almost touching, and look at the artwork.

Mitch points to the wall. "This is their first album. The

one that was on the charts for like three years."

"Uh-huh." I'm purposely trying to play it cool, but inside my heart is slamming against my chest and my thoughts have gone fuzzy.

"And you did the artwork?"

"I was on the team that did it, yes, where I used to work in St. Louis."

"That is so awesome." Mitch turns to me while I continue to look at the picture. I'm beginning to anticipate and crave the electricity zapping between us when we're close. "Have you met them?"

I turn and look up at him. "Yes, I have." I refrain from telling Mitch that I knew Boxwood because the lead singer was the best friend of a victim Donovan had saved. That story is for another time. When we know each other better. When we know each other better? Am I really projecting into the future? "Let me show you something." I gesture to my drafting table. All my #coolNerd work is right out in the open.

Mitch's eyes jump around the table. "#coolNerd? You're doing the artwork for #coolNerd? I knew they had a new album coming out, but this is amazing. You are amazing."

I blush and stutter, "Th-Thank you." Professionally, I have received positive feedback, but never such effusive praise.

"Sorry. I guess that wasn't really smooth, huh?"

"No, it was nice."

"Well, I'm not taking it back. I'm really impressed. You're so talented." He's so free with his feelings. It's refreshing.

I say thank you again and explain my process. "I'm really

inspired by music. Do you want to hear their new album?"

"You have it?"

"I do. Sid Cooper gave it to my boss who gave it to me to help me get the vibe for the artwork."

Mitch looks at the floor and shakes his head in disbelief.

I pull out my phone and grab my earbuds from the table. I plug them in and then hand one of the buds to Mitch. He moves closer to put it in his ear, while I put the other in mine.

"This is going to be the first single released, 'You Are My New Home.'" I start the song.

Mitch immediately closes his eyes and gently moves his head from side to side to the lyrical ballad.

I gaze at him. His lips purse. He's so close. He smells so good. I'd forgotten what it's like to be close to someone. I close my eyes, trying to absorb it all.

Without a word, Mitch slips his arms around my waist and I let him. I reach up, awkward and unsure, and put my hands stiffly on his shoulders. We dance.

Even though every atom in every cell of my body is vibrating at light speed, dancing with Mitch is at the same time easy and comfortable. He begins humming along to the song with perfect pitch.

The song ends, and when I open my eyes, his are open, too, and he's staring down at me.

"Beautiful," he whispers.

Is he commenting on the song or me?

He slowly cups the back of my head with his entire hand and strokes my hair with his thumb.

"Uh." I exhale quickly.

He pulls away slightly, but not before he runs the back of his fingers down the back and then side of my neck.

I shiver from the top of my head down to my toes. We are still connected to the earbuds.

"I'm sorry, that was forward," he whispers while his face moves closer to mine.

He… he's going to kiss me.

"Nuh… no, it's fine." I'm going to let him kiss me…

"Moooommmm!" Loud voices and footsteps thundering down the hall kill the moment.

Mitch and I jump away from each other like we're dodging a moving vehicle. The earbuds yank out of our ears and we both wince.

"Ow!" we both say and retreat to opposite sides of the drafting table.

Van and Shane charge into the room, oblivious. "Can we watch a movie?" They look at me, and then Mitch. Still clueless. Good.

"What time is it? It's a school night," I ask and state in rapid succession, trying to gather my thoughts and interact appropriately.

Shane looks at his phone, holds it up for me to see and makes an exasperated face. "It's only seven thirty"

"Uhm, OK, a short one."

"Yeah, I've got to go." Mitch steps away from the drafting table.

The boys turn on their heels and shout their goodbyes over their shoulders as they leave the room.

"See you Tuesday!" Van adds.

Mitch yells after him, "Don't forget to practice." He gets no response.

The minute the boys are out of earshot, Mitch and I break into spontaneous laughter.

"Busted!"

"Oh. My. God!"

Chapter 8

Van has had seven guitar lessons.

Mitch and I have had seven kid-chaperoned meals, six long conversations, one dance, countless random touches and more than one interrupted almost kiss. I think I may explode.

He's probably figured out that it's always Taco Tuesday and Spaghetti Thursday at our house, because those are the only meals I've served to him. I really need to mix it up. I also need some "alone time" with Mitch.

Today is the eighth lesson, and yes, I am counting.

At quarter to five, there's a knock on the door. I'm not quite used to Mitch not using the doorbell. A knock on the door has become less terrifying, but I must admit, unless everyone I care for is right there with me, I still flinch internally.

Shane and Van tear past my studio, screaming "Mitch!" and "He's here!"

The next thing I hear is a loud ruckus in the kitchen and the word "burgers."

I pad down the hall in my bare feet, slipping my computer glasses on top of my head as I go.

Shane meets me in the hallway and starts pulling me toward the kitchen. "Mom, Mom, look! Look what Mitch brought!"

When I round the corner, there are bags from Five Guys on the counter. Van and Mitch are setting the table. The actual table, not the island. They stop what they're doing, lift the napkins and plates they're holding in their hands above their heads and shout, "Surprise!"

I laugh aloud. "Wow! This is unexpected. So, I'm guessing no Spaghetti Thursday?"

Mitch finishes setting the place setting he had started. "I thought we could mix it up. I figured we should eat now while the food is still warm. Van and I can have the lesson afterward. I hope that's OK?"

"Perfectly. I'm not going to argue with anyone making— or in this case, delivering—dinner. And we're sitting at the table, I see."

"I think it's nice for families to eat at a table," Mitch says with a nod.

As Shane and Van bring the bags of food over and place them it on the plates, Van whispers, "Now he sounds exactly like Dad."

My heart cramps a little. It *is* just like something Donnie would say. I'm both pleased and a little sad. I wish we'd had a few more dinners at the table with him, but I'm also so touched that it was Mitch's idea to do it now.

＊

When Van and Mitch head upstairs for the lesson, Shane and I clean up the kitchen in no time since it's mostly throwing away the bags, wrappers and cups from Five Guys and slipping the plates into the dishwasher. I have about thirty minutes until the lesson is over and I'd like to spend a little time with Mitch. Alone.

I look down at my jeans and T-shirt. This won't do at all. I don't feel very attractive. I was in "work mode" when Mitch arrived, so I wasn't thinking about how I looked, even though I do tend to fix my hair and put on more makeup on days I know he'll be coming over. I head to the master bathroom, run a bath and slip in. My phone is propped up on counter so I can see the clock. I don't want to get too comfortable and fall asleep, but I want to wash off the everyday pressures of the day and get relaxed before I ask Mitch to stay for a while.

I only stay in the tub for ten minutes but it's enough to relax and reset. I towel off quickly then go into my closet to find something to wear. Something that doesn't scream work or Mom. Something pretty. I pick out my nicest bra and panties and settle on a pair of soft black leggings, a black cami and a long, silk, button-up tunic in a blush color, just slightly deeper than my own skin tone. I leave the top four buttons undone, revealing a wee bit more skin. I remain barefoot but dash a little color on my toenails.

While I wait for Van's lesson to be over, I curl up in my comfy club chair in the bay window of the dining room. It occurs to me that I haven't sat here in weeks and weeks. I haven't obsessed as much about Donnie. I haven't missed him as much. Part of that is because I'm focused on my work, but I acknowledge that Mitch is really the impetus. Is my new obsession. It's how I am when I'm around him and why I want to pay more attention to how I look and feel.

Down the hall there is movement and noise.

"Bye, Mitch. See you, Tu-OOOes-day." Van's adolescent voice cracks as he says goodbye.

"See you, bud."

I hear an "oof" like someone being surprise tackled and Shane's sweet voice thanking Mitch for dinner and Mitch telling him what an awesome Lego landspeeder he has. Mitch is phenomenal with my boys.

I watch anxiously for Mitch to appear in the kitchen. After a few more goodbyes, I see him standing next to the kitchen island and looking around. Looking for me?

"Posey?" He raises his voice a bit. He *is* looking for me.

"In here." I wave at him from my perch in the bay window. The lighting is dim with only one floor lamp in the corner next to me.

Mitch squints and then smiles. "There you are."

"Do you want to hang out a bit? Have a beer? It will be your prize for bringing dinner."

"I don't need a prize. It was my pleasure. And yes, I'd love a beer. I subbed today at Sunview High. I didn't know teenagers talked so much when you don't want them to and so little when you do."

Oh my God, he worked all day, got us dinner and then

taught a lesson. He's probably exhausted. I know I would be.

I uncurl my legs to get up and get the beers, but Mitch stops me.

"Don't get up, I'll get the beers and come over there. You look really comfortable." He opens the fridge and pulls out two Pabst Blue Ribbons, in bottles. "PBR in a bottle. Hmmm… hipster—"

"But classy," I say, finishing his sentence.

Mitch pops the tops and walks over to me with a beer in each hand. He hands me mine and then presents his bottle to clink.

"Cheers!" The soft clink fades.

He sits on the ottoman directly in front of me and then scootches it a bit closer. I lean toward him when he places his hand first on the arch of my foot and then slides it up to my knee. His eyes follow his hand. Mine do, too. My stomach flips and all the hairs on my body stand up. It's like my body is craving his touch all on its own.

When his caress stops at my knee, he lifts his head and I raise mine to meet his gaze.

"Hi," he says in a low, direct voice.

"Hi."

"I've been waiting all day to see you. Alone."

"Me, too."

"We need to meet here more often." Mitch waves the beer bottle in his hand around in a circle to indicate the small quiet space.

I smile because he used a pickup line. "Much more often."

I take a sip of my beer and set it down on the table next to me before wiggling my fingers between the fingers of his hand. The one cupping my knee. I rub my thumb along his.

"Posey, do you know why I come to your house two times a week?"

"Of course. To teach Van guitar."

"That's part of it, but, I mean the *real* reason."

"Spaghetti Thursday?"

Mitch guffaws. "Ha! No, and not Taco Tuesday, either."

I shake my head "no," but, really, I know.

Mitch lifts our hands, points one of his fingers, brings it up and presses it right above my left breast over my heart. "You. I come here for you."

Warmth floods my upper body. I'm sure my chest and shoulders flush and my breasts tingle. Wow, just a single touch of his finger and I'm on fire. His eyes never leave mine. I'm caught up.

"Oh." It's the only sound that escapes me.

Mitch continues, "I'd knock on your door every night if I didn't think you'd get sick of me."

Mitch releases my hand, and I slide mine down to his wrist while he reaches up and places his hand on my shoulder.

We move toward each other, so close that I have to tilt my head up to look at him. My gaze moves from his eyes to his gorgeous lips.

"You're welcome here anytime." I husk out in a voice low and full of want.

"I hope you're serious, because I intend to take you up on that offer."

I can't stand staring at his lips and not feeling them on mine, so I rush into him, into his waiting arms.

He scoops me up right to his chest. Our lips crash and tangle. A manifestation of our long pent-up desire. Somehow, Mitch maneuvers himself so that *he's* sitting in the chair and I am sitting in his lap, cradled in his capable arms.

I immediately wish we had done this sooner. What had I been waiting for? Why? That was easily answered. Guilt over Donnie. And fear. And one more thing… Mitch's age.

I pull away panting. Mitch's smile is huge. "Is this OK?" I ask.

"OK? I've been waiting four weeks, twenty-three hours and fifty-nine minutes to kiss you."

Come on! Is he for real? "That's pretty precise."

"I may be off by a minute or two. No, really. You opened that door last month and I knew. I knew someday I'd be kissing you. The way you looked, smelled, your eyes and your kids. I mean, they are great kids. I was taken in by everything about you."

"I had on cutoffs and a messy bun."

"You looked perfect to me."

"You're saying all the right things."

Mitch cups my face in his hands and kisses my eyelids, my cheeks and finally my lips. First, gently biting my lower lip and then crashing into both. I reciprocate with equal fervor and open to Mitch's tongue sweeping across mine in long, panty-drenching suckles. We continue for long minutes.

I haven't made out in a very, very long time because after you sleep with someone, you rarely make out like hormonal teenagers anymore. God, I love making out.

I find myself straddling Mitch, his hands under my silk shirt, palms on my sides with his thumbs grazing under my breasts, just barely touching them. His erection is firm and present, and I thrust my core against it through the barrier of our clothing.

This will become more than making out if it continues much longer. And the kids are right down the hall. I reluctantly press my palms flat on Mitch's chest—his chest that is as firm as that other part of him beneath me—and push away. Our lips stay locked until I'm too far away and the kiss is finally broken.

We are both "ran a 5K in record time" out of breath.

"Mitch."

"Posey."

"I don't want to stop, but I think maybe…"

"Yeah, I know, too fast."

"It wouldn't be right…" I tilt my head toward the boys' rooms.

"Oh, it would be right. It would be so right."

I sigh, frustrated, and then giggle. "I know, but—"

"Yeah, I don't want to rush this, but if I have to go…" He gives me a big, sad panda frown.

I frown right back. "You do."

"If I have to go, I have two questions. I'm going to ask one now and one later."

"OK."

"Go out with me Saturday night? I'm in a new band. We have a gig. I'd love if you'd go with me and then spend some more time with me—alone." Mitch's eyes sparkle with anticipation.

He wants to spend more time with me.

"I'd love to."

We slowly disentangle ourselves from each other and the club chair. When we're both standing, I look down at "my spot" in the chair. I don't think I'll be able to think of it as a place to be sad again.

After he gathers his guitar and bag, I walk Mitch to the door. We linger. He kisses me long and slow while pressing me against the doorjamb. I watch him walk away, appreciating the way his back muscles strain against his T-shirt and how his hips move with each stride. I don't go inside until he blows me a kiss before ducking into his truck. I mime catching it and hold it to my chest.

OK, I admit it. That was corny. Mitch blowing a kiss and me catching it. It's something that never would have happened with Donnie. He was a serious guy who didn't show his emotions easily.

But you know what? I love it. Mitch's openess. I love every silly, corny, honest thing Mitch does, because it makes me feel alive again after years of feeling defeated and cynical.

I've come so far in two years since I moved to Sunview.

I am finally beginning to look, if not feel, a bit like the old Posey. The one that capably ran her world and a couple other people's.

No, I am not the old Posey.

I am a brand-new Posey.

Chapter 9

One of the reasons I moved to Sunview was because my parents lived close by. Let me rephrase: the *only* reason I moved to Sunview is because I couldn't make a decision on my own after Donnie died and my parents had retired in the next town over from Sunview and insisted I move closer to them. I'd be living there, except Sunview has a better school district. They found this house. They moved me down here. They kept me sane in the beginning.

They live just close enough that I feel like I have a support system and just far enough away that it's pretty impossible to "drop by." Really, I have nothing to complain about, they always text or call before they come over. Plus, they'd take any opportunity to come stay with the boys.

I called my mother first thing Friday morning.

"Mom, could you and Dad come stay with the boys tomorrow night? I know it's short notice."

"Well, sure honey. What's going on? Something at work?

"No, I'm actually going out to see a friend's band and then go on a date with him after."

"Really, sweetheart? That's so good. Who is he? How do you know him?"

"His name is Mitch. He's actually Van's guitar teacher."

"Oh, yes, you've mentioned him."

"The thing is… he's young. Younger than me. A lot younger than me."

"I'm older than your dad by three years."

"Yeah." I hesitate. "This is a bit more than three years."

"How much more?"

"Uh… I'm not really sure."

She's silent on the other end of the call for a moment, then effusively says in a voice high, bright and full of hope, "I'll be happy to meet him. I'm just so thrilled you're going to something other than a work or school meeting."

I swear I can hear her smile.

***

I've torn through my closet and come up with an outfit I think will work for tonight. Skinny jeans, leopard boots, hoop earrings and a black cold-shoulder top.

Mitch's band is playing at a bar down at the beachfront. I don't know much about it except he said it was called Snapback. Sounds like a sports bar. I hope I'm not overdressed.

I've just finished putting on my mascara when the doorbell rings. The door opens followed by a huge ruckus of excited voices—my mom, my dad and both the boys—all talking at once.

"How can you grow that fast in one week?"

"Van, how's guitar going?"

As I walk down the hall, I make out Van's answer.

"Mitch is teaching me how to play Pink Floyd and Zeppelin and—"

"Hey," I call to them as I reach the kitchen. From the foyer, four heads swing to look at me. Four pairs of eyes look me up and down and then up again. Four mouths open in surprise.

My father smiles broadly and walks to meet me with arms outstretched. "Posey, sweetheart, you look beautiful!" He puts his hands on my shoulders.

"Thank you, Dad."

My father pulls me in for a hug—a hug full of meaning. He's so happy to see me in something other than a long gray cardigan and sweatpants, I'm sure.

My mother joins him. She reaches up to touch my hair above my ears. "You cut your hair. It's adorable."

"Thanks, Mom."

The boys have come in with them and chirp, "Whoa! You look so pretty, Mom."

It's like a Posey appreciation party in my kitchen.

The sudden knock on the door causes me to jump. I don't think it will ever be a sound I'm comfortable with, even if I'm quite sure of who is doing the knocking.

The heads and eyes swing away from me and to the door.

"I bet that's Mitch," I say, solving the mystery of the hand at the end of the knock.

Van and Shane scramble to the door, pushing and shoving to be the first one there.

Van opens the door and he and Shane take their turn greeting him with the oh-so-cool handshake and bro-hug combination. Shane lingers in hugging Mitch. My heart pounds a bit harder. Shane had just turned eight when Donnie died. He didn't get enough hugs from his dad. Not nearly enough.

The boys flank Mitch and "escort" him to my parents and me.

Mitch's eyes lock onto mine. If he's aware there's anyone else in the room, he's not letting on. When he's directly in front of me, he whispers, "Wow! Posey. You... you look amazing. I mean, you always look amazing, but you look... Wow!"

I blush from head to toe.

Mitch leans down and kisses my cheek. He's still acting as if we are the only two people in the room. For that matter, I am, too.

My father clears his throat. "Ahem."

It's that subtle cue that pulls my attention from Mitch's gorgeous, scruffy face, sexy eyes, hair... lips.

"Oh, my gosh, yes, Mitch, these are my parents, Charles and Caroline Spence. Mom, Dad, this is Mitch Morgan. He's Van's guitar teacher..."

"And Posey's date tonight." Mitch finishes the introduction. "It's great to meet you both." He shakes my mother's hand, and I swear she sighs. Then he shakes my dad's hand and pulls him in for a hug, like he did with the boys. My father's face opens in surprise, and then he breaks out in a huge grin. I hear him guffaw once.

"Good to meet you, too, Mitch."

My dad and Mitch discuss where he's taking me tonight.

My mother and I discuss the boys' bedtime and that she should order pizza for dinner.

It's clear that neither Mitch nor I are attending to our respective conversations, because our eyes are not engaged fully with the other people in the room, but instead are constantly searching for each other.

Mitch breaks up the discourse. "Well, I think we should be going, Posey. We need to get a table and something to eat before I have to play."

Mom and Dad walk us to the door. Van and Shane have already gone to the family room to play a video game and shout their goodbyes over their shoulders.

When they close the door behind us, I can make out my parents loud whispering and my mother saying "handsome."

Mitch and I stop on the porch, turn and smile at each other, and laugh simultaneously. He shakes his head.

Between laughs I comment, "Meeting the parents…"

"Yeah," Mitch agrees. "Never gets less awkward. No matter how old you are."

There's that word again. Old. How old is he? I know he's been to college. So at least twenty-two? Oh God, don't let him be twenty-two. That would be too young. That would be wrong.

Chapter 10

"I hope this is OK?" Mitch asks as we head into a local pizza place on the strip by the beach. It's called Princiotti's. It's supposed to be really good. Real New York–style pizza. Where I used to live, in St. Louis, pizza is a hot topic. There's a very particular kind there, obviously called St. Louis style. Thin crust, cut in squares with gooey cheese that sticks to the roof of your mouth. You can't get it anywhere else in the world.

With my mind still rhapsodizing about pizza as a distraction, I reply, "Sure, I've wanted to bring the kids here."

"It's one of my favorite places to eat. And Snapback is close, so we can get there in time for the sound check."

"You're playing at a sports bar?" I tease. I didn't take Mitch as the sporto type, although he's fit enough that he could be. We've just never discussed sports.

"Yes," Mitch bugs his eyes out and tilts his head in response to my teasing. "But the band doesn't play in the bar. There's an outdoor patio with a stage for those who don't need to have their eyes constantly glued to an eighty-inch flat-screen."

The hostess shows us to our booth and hands us menus.

"Do you like sports?" It's one of those things I don't know about him and maybe I should.

"Baseball's OK, but we don't really have a good team here."

In St. Louis everybody had Cardinals fever whether you liked sports or not. Donnie was a huge fan.

Mitch continues, "Football's a little better. I'd watch a Gators game if it was on and I wasn't doing something else. So yeah, I like it OK. I'm not, like, a huge obsessive, sit on the couch on a Saturday kind of guy."

I'm relieved. "I was sort of thinking that, but there's still a lot we don't know about each other."

Mitch reaches across the table and squeezes my hand. "We have plenty of time." He holds me with his jade green gaze. I nod. Plenty of time. Donnie used to say that, too.

"Ahem." We are so wrapped up in each other, I don't even notice the waitress standing at the end of the booth until she clears her throat.

Mitch and I jump away from each other, releasing our hands and looking up at her. Interruptions are becoming more and more annoying. Mitch rolls his eyes and laughs. The waitress must think we're nuts.

Mitch orders the pizza, but not before asking me if his choice is OK with me. He asks me if I want a beer, and when I say yes, he orders two draft light beers. This is not the kind of place with a large selection of craft beers. They have regular, light and nonalcoholic. That's it.

We eat and talk and debate the merits of New York–

versus Chicago- versus St. Louis–style pizza. Mitch fakes being appalled when I describe the flat cracker-like pizza of my hometown. I find out he is originally from a suburb of Chicago and a lover of deep dish. We agree that the pizza we're eating is a good compromise between the two. I also discover he moved here to go to college. I'm just about to ask when that was when Mitch looks at his watch.

"Hey, we gotta go! Sound check is in five. You are extremely distracting, Ms. Garrett." Mitch throws some money on the table with the check.

Ms. Garrett. He said Ms., not Mrs. I'd never thought of myself that way, until now.

***

We turn left as we exit Princiotti's and Mitch detours to grab his guitar out of his truck. Walking hand in hand, we arrive at Snapback in short order—literally one hundred feet.

"Wow, you were right. The bar is close."

The place is packed with people waiting to get in and others spilling out onto the sidewalk as they exit.

Mitch greets the bouncer and says, "She's with the band."

I giggle when the bouncer lets us right in.

We weave our way through the crowd and the noise of the multiple televisions blaring games I can only assume are being played on the West Coast. The air is close and tight. I finally exhale when we make it through to a large patio area facing the beach. There's a stage to the left and tables and chairs to the right. Even though the band doesn't play for a while, the tables are filling up.

"Uhm, let's grab a table. I need to get up there." Mitch points to the stage. We find an empty one in the middle near the front by the sound booth. Mitch pulls out a chair and I sit. He kisses me on the cheek. "I'll be back after sound check," he whispers in my ear.

On his way up to the stage, he stops a waitress and points back to me. She reaches up and runs her hand down his arm. I don't like it. Thank God, Mitch shrugged her touch away.

The waitress walks straight up to the table. "Mitch said to get you whatever you want. So, what do you want?" She's less than hospitable.

"PBR?"

"We only got that in cans. That OK?"

"Sure."

She smiles broadly. "You probably remember PBR from before it was trendy." Her voice is rife with sarcasm.

I just smile and huff out an equally sarcastic, "Yeah, right." Bitch!

Actually, I do remember when PBR was just the cheapest beer you could buy, and Donnie and I were living on a rookie cop's salary. She's right. It wasn't cool then, but that waitress doesn't need to, not so subtly, comment on my age.

The band checks the sound, making an adjustment here and there. They sound good. Their music is the driving guitar rock that Van likes and is learning from Mitch. Mitch lifts his head from his guitar to sing into his mike. Every time he sings he looks straight down at me.

Waitress chick comes back with my beer. Slams it down

so that foam fountains out of the top and says, "That'll be five ninety-nine."

I pull some cash out from my jeans.

Suddenly Mitch's voice over the speaker stops all the noise in the bar.

"Stacy, I told you to run a tab for me. Put anything Posey wants on it."

Every woman standing in the bar sighs audibly. Someone whispers, "Who's Posey?"

I turn red with embarrassment.

"Fine!" Stacy whispers angrily. "Posey? *That's* your name?" More snottiness as she twists her face up in disgust.

I put my money back in my pocket. "Yes, and now that Mitch has told everyone here"—I smile overly sweetly and run my hand through my hair—"I'm sure you won't forget."

Mitch hops off the stage when the band and sound technician are sure they have all the levels right for tonight. He makes a beeline to our table. The rest of the band follows him. I guess I'm meeting the band now.

"Posey, meet my band. Dave plays guitar, Dave the bass, and Hermione on the drums."

I shake hands with everyone. "So nice to meet you."

"We're glad to meet you. Mitch talks about you all the time, but since we've never seen you we though he was making you up."

"No, I'm real."

"You sure are," Mitch declares as he sits in the chair next to me, runs his hand down my arm and squeezes my hand.

Three girls slowly make their way to our table. Dave,

Dave and Hermione's girlfriends introduce themselves and welcome me to the "band widows" table.

I wince internally. Better a band widow than a real one.

Mitch slides an arm around my waist as he pulls himself closer and whispers in my ear, "You OK?"

"Yeah, yes. 'Widow' is just a word. I know they don't mean to be hurtful."

"They don't know about your past. I didn't let them know."

"I figured. It's OK, really."

Mitch kisses me softly on the neck below my ear. Right there for everyone to see.

The Daves and Hermione greet their girlfriends with hugs and kisses. After I learn that Jane is guitar Dave's girl, Gwen, bass Dave's girl, and Rhonda, Hermione's girlfriend, they sit. Stacy comes over to get their drink orders. It doesn't escape my notice that she does so without any snark or commentary. She's actually friendly to them.

As Stacy takes the drink orders, Hermione lifts her chin at Mitch.

Looks like it's time for them to play. He scoots away from the table, but not before leaning in again and saying, "Be back soon." He kisses me. This time right on the lips. I kiss him right back.

When he's gone, I turn my attention back to the table. All eyes are on me, and Stacy's not just staring, she's glaring at me.

She turns abruptly and marches off, but not until she says to everyone but me, "So, if there's nothing else, I'll get your drinks."

I wait until she's out of range before saying, "Wow, Stacy actually likes you guys."

Jane answers, "Sure, we're here a lot. Why? Was Stacy snarky to you?"

"That's a nice way of putting it."

"Aaah!" Rhonda chimes in. "That's probably because she's had a thing for Mitch *for-ever*. I think he was drunk on New Year's and kissed her, and she thinks it meant something."

I must have frowned because Gwen reaches over and grabs my hand. "Posey, it didn't mean a thing to Mitch. If you didn't know it, we've nicknamed him 'The Monk' because he's never brought a girl to a gig, ever. Sure, girls throw themselves at him all the time, but he never responds. I actually almost fell out of my chair when he kissed you. That was fucking hot!"

"I can't believe he's never brought a girl"—I leave out the word *friend*—"to a gig before."

"Nope, you're the first," Rhonda adds, confirming it.

"Someone in his past must have hurt him real bad," Gwen says.

The band widows all nod in agreement.

I have an important question. "And how long has the band been together?"

"About three years."

"After college."

"Forever." They answer in unison.

So, if the band has been together since college and that was three years ago, Mitch must be about… twenty-fi—

"Ladies and gentlemen!" Mitch's amplified voice interrupts my rudimentary mental math.

"We are…" Mitch and the band take their places on stage and a large banner drops behind them: *The Band That Must Not Be Named.*

Mitch and everyone in the venue whisper-shout, "Bandemort!"

I laugh. Very clever.

Rhonda shouts across the table, "That was Hermione's idea! She figured if she had Hermione for a handle, she had a right to choose that name for the band. Plus, they're all ginormous *Harry Potter* nerds." Another thing I didn't know about Mitch. I'm learning more about him by the minute.

The band has the place rocking. Watching Mitch in action, I can see he's ridiculously talented and this is clearly his passion. He's as good as Sid Cooper from #coolNerd. I can't help the shiver that runs up my spine each time he turns his head and sings directly to me.

Jane, Rhonda and Gwen tease me. "Are you picking up how he looks right at you every time he sings the words *love* and *baby*?"

Sheepishly I answer, "Yeah." I can't begin to describe the way I feel when he does.

Rhonda leans in to me to avoid yelling. "We're so glad he met you. He's a much happier camper these days."

I learn from the girls that Mitch had garnered interest from a couple of touring bands to join them recently. He turned them down.

I should spend more time with these ladies. They're like

a Mitch Morgan Wikipedia page.

The band plays for an hour and half with no break. They do cover songs with the occasional original song. One of them is titled "Cul-de-sac Love." Mitch dedicates it to "my special girl from Juniper Court." My heart is so full. I must confess, I'm falling hard.

After two encores, the band leaves the stage for good. Mitch wastes no time making his way back to me. He has a beer in hand and is mopping sweat from his face and hair, and I can't wait to be close to him. Without a second thought, I push away from the table and navigate my way through the crowd to meet him halfway. I rush into his arms, spilling his beer a little, and look into his stunning, sweaty face. Damp from perspiration, he smells like sandalwood and warmth and dare I think it... sex.

Mitch laughs. "Well, hi! Did you miss me?"

"Yeah, I did." I didn't know it until I said it. Up onstage, he was right there in front of me, but the more he sang and the longer he wasn't right next to me, the more I missed him.

It can wait no longer, I want to feel his lips on mine. I reach up and twist my fingers into his wet hair at the nape of his neck. I push up on my toes and kiss him, slow and soft, and then fast and deep. So deep, my core floods with heat and desire. I need to be with him in a less populated place. A place with no chance of interruptions.

If the physical reaction his body is having to my kiss is any indication, he wants the same thing.

Mitch pulls away. "Oh God, Posey, babe... let's get out of here."

He called me babe. "OK."

"I gotta get my guitar."

"I gotta get my purse." Our directives are clear and meaningful.

I turn and head back to the table to get my purse and say goodbye to the girls. As I do, I overhear a group of men congratulating Mitch.

"Man, that was awesome!"

"When are you playing again?"

"Dude, didn't know you were with a cougar!"

I look up to see Mitch's reaction to the cougar comment. He's shaking hands and nodding as he moves away from the praise of a group of college guys.

Was he agreeing with them?

Chapter 11

Mitch and I make small talk while we caress and tangle our hands together on the center console of his truck on the way over to Mitch's place. It isn't far from the bar, maybe seven blocks at most. Once he parks, we're out of the car and racing hand in hand across the parking lot in record time.

I stop suddenly. "You live here?"

"Yes," Mitch says, a little frustrated, and tugs me forward.

We're at the edge of a little bridge that spans a canal. On the other side is an adorable house. It's located on a small strip of land between the canal and the intercoastal waterway. It's one of many tall, narrow, two-story, wood frame homes.

"You live on the intercoastal?"

"Yes," Mitch says again but doesn't stop to explain or elaborate. He finally herds me across the bridge to the house. Mitch directs me to the outside stairs that lead to the upper level. "Up here."

I follow him up. How can a struggling musician afford a

waterfront apartment on the intercoastal?

Reaching the top landing, Mitch releases my hand. I gasp at how beautiful the view is, but only for a second. My focus shifts from the breathtaking vista to the sound of a key turning a lock and the breathtaking man I'm with. I admire Mitch's strong shoulders and arms opening the door to me. He smiles and waves me inside with a chivalrous bow of the head.

I don't go in. Instead, I charge into his arms, back him against the doorjamb and thrust my hands into his hair to bring his lips to mine. We kiss. Short, frantic kisses. One landing milliseconds after the next. As our kisses lengthen and deepen, Mitch backs me up against the opposite side of the doorjamb. He firmly holds me with one hand at the nape of my neck and the other cupping my hip. His long, capable fingers grasp the top of my butt while his thumb skates down my hipbone.

We stay in the doorway only moments before we twirl and tangle, our bodies moving like molecules that have been kept apart too long and finally crash together and fuse. I tear at the buttons on his shirt. He, in turn, pushes my jacket over my shoulders and down my arms. He flings it away to who knows where. I've managed to get his shirt off and start tugging on the sleeveless T-shirt partly tucked into his jeans that are straining under the pressure of a growing erection. All the time we are walking backward and sideways, a tornado of passion trying to touch down.

Mitch pulls his lips away, but we are still touching, grasping, caressing. Anything to get closer.

Mitch rests his forehead on mine and asks, earnestly, "Is this OK?"

"Yes."

"Really? You? You want this? Want me?"

"Yes, Mitch. Yes. So much."

No other confirmation is needed. Mitch's lips crash down on mine. He grabs my knee and pulls it up around his waist. I jump slightly and hook my other leg around him. I can feel his hardness and I slide against it greedily. Mitch's arms encircle me completely. He carries me into the next room. He's half naked, and touching the ripples and bulges of his back muscles sends scorching sensations to my breasts and sensitive places even lower.

Mitch lowers me to the floor. Never breaking contact, we give minimal directions to get out of our clothes.

"Here."

"Over my head."

"Just pull the end of belt."

It would be comical if we weren't so desperate with want.

Finally down to the last scraps of clothing, we stand face to face, millimeters apart, and everything slows. The air we breathe is thick and moves between us languidly. Mitch drags down the straps of my bra with deliberate movements of his fingers. Fingers, deft at coaxing music from a stringed instrument, are now playing me. Making the cells in my skin sing. He unhooks the bra and my breasts tumble out. And just as quickly, he catches them, cupping them. He rakes his thumbs across each nipple and I arch into him.

Mitch bends down and trails deep, suckling kisses down

the side of my neck and across my collarbone. He moves further down and brings my cupped breast to his mouth. His breath on it causes my nipple to tighten painfully. The pleasant discomfort builds when he pulls the whole of my nipple between his lips, tugging and laving it. Flames shoot to my core. I arch into him, only my panties and his boxer briefs separating us.

"Oh, sweet Jesus, Posey," Mitch husks deeply, moving from one breast to another. "Have mercy."

With my head in a swirl but needing more, I cup Mitch's relentless stiffness and massage his balls. He moans, and I moan with him as he powers his suckling of my breast.

I stroke him up and down and with each one, I ache to feel all of him. With that I slide my fingers inside the elastic of his briefs and push them down. Mitch moans again. His lips leave my body. He stands upright, takes his briefs off and spins me around so my back is to his naked front. His erection presses and pulses on my lower back.

Mitch slides a hand around my front and inside my panties. His fingers walk downward until they find my clit. He strokes left, right and circles and circles. My lower abs contract and I pitch forward, sure I'm about to come.

Mitch stops, retreats and whispers, "Shh, not yet. I got you."

He hooks his fingers onto my panties and drags them down my legs as he kneels and artfully trails kisses down my back, ending at the top of my ass. I step out of my panties pooling around my feet.

Half kneeling behind me, Mitch spins me so I'm facing

him, but he is facing my most sensitive of areas. He kisses my thigh, and with just his breath that close to where I want all of him causes me to grasp his shoulder to steady myself.

Mitch looks up at me and I look down. There is no mistaking the message we're giving each other.

"Posey?" I've never heard Mitch's voice deeper, more penetrating.

"Mitch." I say his name instead of *yes*.

"I need you in my bed, right now."

"I need to be there."

In a swift well-orchestrated move, Mitch scoops me up, cradles me against him, walks to the bed and gently places me on it. I'm so caught up, I didn't take notice of anything around us. This could be a bed anywhere. I couldn't care less as long as I'm in it with him.

I expect Mitch to slip in next to me, but he doesn't. He's over me. All of him over all of me, kissing me long, slow with his tongue sweeping across mine. I try to rock my needy core against his hardness, but he shifts and kisses down my body, stopping briefly to draw my nipple into his mouth and kiss between my lower abdomen and hip bones.

Then he reaches his target, he Heexhales and my clit pulses. It's already vibrating and ready. His tongue touches it lightly.

"Oh my God," I moan.

Again, the left, right, circle, circle, left, right... just like he did with his fingers, but now it's his hot, wet tongue. A slow building, warm tingling overtakes me. I reach down and grasp his hair.

He stops and I cry out, "Please!"

I know what he's doing. He's edging me. Closer and closer. Stopping my orgasm just as I'm about to let go, but I need this release.

Blessedly, Mitch continues. As his tongue works his magic below, he reaches up and pinches and releases my nipples in synchrony. I lose my mind. I can't continue. He licks me up and down and then circles deeply and powerfully, sucking my burning clit. I arch as every muscle in my body contracts, stiffening until I'm unable to move. He flattens his tongue and holds it firm against me and I come. Hard. Panting with each wave. He stays where he is, drinking me in. Humming with pleasure.

Descending my climax, I'm breathing hard but want more. I tug on his hair and shoulders. When he brings his face up to mine, I roll him on his back.

"Do... do you have protection?" My turn to make him lose himself.

"Yes, in the drawer." He points to the nightstand on the right.

I reach in and feel around. My hand lands on the familiar foil-wrapped shape. I rip it open with my teeth.

He laughs, but stops and groans when I sit back, grasp his cock and stroke it up and down a few times while grazing my thumb across its plush pink head. I roll the condom on with care.

"You're killing me, babe," he groans.

In answer to his plea, I straddle him and encircle the base of his erection in my palm and guide him into the wetness he evoked. I moan as he stretches and fills me. I gasp at the familiar but long denied sensation. I believed I would never make love again. I stifle a sob that sneaks up on me.

Mitch cups my face in his hands. "Are you OK?"

I swipe at my eyes. "Yes, oh, yes, I'm just…" I was going to say overwhelmed, but instead I say, "happy." I am happy. I never thought I'd be really, truly happy again, either.

We rock into each other, sighing and humming, in perfect rhythm. As it builds, we begin thrusting into crescendo, harder, faster. So intense, our kisses end, but our mouths open still millimeters apart.

The build reaches its peak and I contract around him. He in turn arches his head back, his mouth opens wide and his eyes close tight. He falls apart beneath me and comes a moment after I do. I'm flooded with his warmth and pleasure crashes and crashes inside me until it devolves into tiny waves lapping at the shore.

Chapter 12

Mitch must be exhausted.

I've gotten up, found his button-up and put it on, gone into the kitchen and made some coffee, and am now watching the sunrise from the doorway of the balcony off his room. He hasn't moved an inch.

I take a sip of coffee and watch the world wake up across the intercoastal. Birds launch themselves into the sky. The seagulls are being especially noisy, diving and fighting over fish. I wonder if it will wake Mitch up. I take another sip and rub my hand on my opposite arm and my foot against my leg when a breeze blows in.

I can't stop my mind from going back to what that guy in the bar said. *Cougar*. I look over my shoulder at Mitch. Sound asleep, lips pursed and pouty, one arm over his face, the other resting across his rippled abs.

Am I a cougar? I guess I am, because I'm older than Mitch, but the word *cougar* connotes that I only see him as fresh meat. My latest kill. I don't feel that way about Mitch at all. I like him. Really like him and his heart. Being around

Mitch, and now being with him, I'm calmer than I've been since… well, since I lost Donnie.

Donnie. I'll never stop loving him. I'll never stop missing him. I see him every day in the faces of Van and Shane. But he left me.

Maybe it's not right, but it doesn't feel wrong.

Mitch's arm slips down from his face, and he reaches out to my side of the bed. His eyes open suddenly, and he searches the room until he sees me looking over my shoulder at him.

"Hey, you," he says, his voice all warm, rough and bedroomy.

"Hey," I say back, trying to match his tone.

He pats the bed. "I think you are much too far away."

I turn toward him. "Do you?"

"Yes. I require you to come back here."

"Require me?"

"I think that's the best way to put it."

I saunter toward the bed, stand next to it and look down at him. I take another sip of coffee and then hand it to him.

He takes a sip. "Hmmm, warm, creamy and just a little bit sweet. Just the way I like it." He takes one more sip, places the coffee cup on the nightstand, and takes my hand and gently tugs me down to him.

I cuddle against his chest, and he strokes my arm. I reflexively make a purring, humming sound. Like a cat.

A cat.

A cougar.

I slide a hand across Mitch's firm and hairless chest, and turn my head slightly to look into his face.

He gazes down at me.

I bite my lip and then press my lips into a line.

"What's up, Posey? You're thinking too hard. What's going on in that head?"

"How did you know I was thinking about something?"

"You were up before dawn. You have a look on your face like you want to ask me something. And there is this little look of... pain, almost, in your eyes."

I swallow a couple of times. "I hope this isn't... I... last night, at the bar. I heard one of the guys you were talking to call me a cougar."

"So?"

"Exactly how old are you?"

He sighs. "I knew this would come up at some point. Posey, I'm twenty-five, twenty-six in a few months."

Jesus, he was thirteen when I gave birth to Van!

I start to shift away, but Mitch holds me tighter, not letting me. He pins me with his eyes, all sincerity. "You know that doesn't matter to me."

I wonder why it matters to me. Why I'm so worried it's wrong.

"It doesn't? But what about...?" I'm about to ask him about what others think and kids and the future, but I don't get a chance because Mitch shakes his head no. He cups my face in one of his hands, rubs his thumb along my jawline and kisses me deeply. It scrambles my thoughts.

When he stops kissing me, he leans his forehead against mine. "I've always liked cats," he whispers with a smirk in his voice. Again, I purr. He has a way of taming my anxiety.

Mitch fingers the collar of the button-up I'm currently wearing.

"Let's stop talking about cougars and other people."

"OK."

"I'd rather talk about how good my shirt looks on you and how much better it would look off you."

I sink down into the bed and giggle as he unbuttons my shirt, delivering a tiny kiss behind each button that's freed.

No more talk right now.

Chapter 13

Mitch and I are parked down the street and around the corner from Juniper Court. We look like detectives staking out a suspect as we stare at my house.

"So how are we going to do this?" Mitch questions me.

I had planned to go home last night. I had planned to be in my own bedroom this morning when the boys woke up. Those plans went deliciously sideways, but now I must get back in without them knowing. I texted my mother and father last night and told them to go to sleep, that I'd be home very late. It's not uncommon for them to spend the night in the guest room when they come over. My mom texted me a "Sure" and a smiley emoji. Damn those kids for showing her emojis!

"I'll sneak in. Go to my room and change."

Mitch moans in frustration before reaching over and pulling me to him. "Now I'm thinking of you changing clothes."

"Stop." I press my hands against his chest, but with little resistance.

I kiss him quickly and then scramble out the door. "Wait about fifteen, twenty minutes and then come over."

"Yes, ma'am." Mitch salutes me as I get out and trot down the street.

As I approach the door, I can't hear a thing from the house. Not unusual for this early on a Sunday morning.

After punching in the code to turn off the alarm to the house, I creep in. I'm able to sneak down the hall and into my room undetected. I change into some soft, gray jersey sweatpants, a #coolNerd baseball shirt and slouchy socks. A quick glance in the mirror reveals my mussed hair and smudged makeup. Yep, I pretty much look like I do every Sunday. Except the mussing and smudging are from a night of amazing sex. I catch myself smiling. Better calm that down or I'll give myself away.

As I open my bedroom door to go to the kitchen and start coffee and breakfast, I startle. My mother is standing directly in front of me. Completely dressed. Hair perfect.

"Posey? Did you have a good evening?"

I smile. "Yes, I had a really good time." Better than you know, Mom.

"I thought so, you must have gotten in really late. I went to bed a little after midnight." She's totally digging for information.

I turn and head down the hall to stop the inquisition.

"Yeah, it was a couple hours after that." Technically, I'm not lying. Sure, it was more than a couple hours, but it was after she went to bed.

No sooner do I get the water and coffee in the coffee

maker—all the while avoiding my mother's gaze—than the kids rush in.

"Hey, Grandma. Hey, Mom. Where's Mitch?"

"He'll be here soon."

"We thought he'd be here already," Van says.

I look over my shoulder. My mother's jaw drops. I guess she wasn't prepared for the kids to be expecting him to be here. Or that we'd all be so familiar and accustomed to him being in our house.

"Is Mitch here a lot?"

Shane pipes up, completely innocently. "Yeah, almost all the time."

My mother opens her mouth and I know she's about to ask more questions, but there's a loud knock at the front door.

I jump slightly.

Van and Shane rush to the door and greet Mitch. They escort him, or more accurately pull him, into the kitchen.

I finish pouring the cup of coffee I turned away from my mother to get, then set it down in front of her. She thanks me, all the while assessing the interactions between Mitch, the boys and myself. I can see in her eyes she's trying to figure out how attached we all are.

"Good morning, Mrs. Spence."

"Good morning, Mitch. Nice to see you again."

I've turned back to the coffee maker, sure I won't be able to keep a telling smile off my face.

Not looking at him, I ask, "Mitch? Coffee?"

Mitch enthusiastically answers, "Yes!" He makes his way

over to me, stands right next to me and slips his arm around my waist, cupping my hip.

Mitch leans in and kisses me on the head. "Good morning. Again," he whispers.

"Shh!" I point a thumb behind me at my mother.

My father pads out from the guest room, dressed in an open bathrobe, white T-shirt, plaid boxers and black socks.

"What's all the noise? Oh, I didn't know we had company!" He quickly closes his bathrobe and ties the belt.

Mitch pours and delivers a cup of coffee to him as he sits at the kitchen counter next to Mom.

"Good morning, sir. How are you?"

My still sleepy and somewhat baffled dad rubs his eyes, like he's not quite sure he's seeing what he's seeing, "Uh, good morning, Mitch."

Mitch takes control of breakfast before I can even get started.

"I'm thinking waffles, scrambled eggs and bacon. Van and Shane, can you set the table?"

"Yup," they answer. Without complaint the boys gather plates and silverware and get on the task.

Mom volunteers to help and is soon behind the counter with Mitch. Mitch hands me a cup of coffee and shoos me out, directing me to sit with my dad. Mitch and my mother act as a well-oiled machine, preparing breakfast. They chatter as if they'd known each other for years. Mom tells him to stop calling them Mr. and Mrs. Spence and call them Charles and Caroline. My heart goes a bit mushy.

My slow-to-rise-in-the-morning father attends to all the

breakfast making impassively as he sips his coffee.

But he finally speaks. "How was your evening?"

"Uh, good. It was really good." Really, really good!

"What did you do?"

I tell him about dinner and Mitch's gig, but stop there.

In all actuality, I can't stop thinking about spending the night in Mitch's arms. In Mitch's bed.

Chapter 14

Tuesday and Thursday lessons have turned into Friday and Saturday dates with Sunday brunches and Mitch at the house all the time. I'm surprised how perfectly fine with it, thrilled with it, I am. My kids expect him to be at the house and are disappointed when he isn't. I think he even got my parents' phone number after we all had breakfast together.

He spends the night.

His toothbrush is in my bathroom.

I think we need to talk.

Van and Mitch have finished their Thursday lesson, and they are coming downstairs. I'm in my studio, putting the last touches on the #coolNerd album cover and associated ads, when Valley calls and asks if Shane and Van can spend the night because there's no school tomorrow.

She must have been reading my mind. I love my children, but I desperately need to talk to Mitch alone. We're moving at a pretty rapid rate and I'm anxious. Are we on the same page?

"Really, Valley? They can spend the night?"

"Posey, I'll even feed them dinner. It's clear you need to have an evening alone with Mitch."

"How do you know?"

"Well, he's been over at your house almost every night, but I know all too well how hard it is to let loose with kids in the house."

I visualize her winking at me.

"More than you know. Plus, I think Mitch and I need to talk."

"Uh-oh."

"It's nothing bad. I don't think…"

"But?"

"But… Mitch is a lot younger than I am."

"Oh, I know." She draws out each one of the words and once again I visualize a wink with a seductive pucker of Valley's lips this time.

"Annnnd… I just wonder if we want the same things. Long-term."

"I don't know about that, but short-term it appears you're both getting what you want."

"VAL-ley!"

"Just send the kids over."

The boys pack up in nanoseconds and fly out the door and over to Valley's house. Mitch and I stand in the doorway waving. I remind them to behave and mind Valley.

"K!" they shout back, loud enough for everyone in the cul-de-sac to hear.

The door barely shuts behind us when Mitch pushes me up against it firmly, takes my face in his hands and kisses me.

It is not sweet. It is not cute. It is deep and probing and sets my thighs on fire. My nipples harden and my core clenches. My lips reciprocate but I'm so overwhelmed, I can't move my arms. They just dangle at my sides, heavy and unmoving. He may have actually paralyzed me with his kiss.

Mitch breaks the kiss and leans his forehead against mine. We are both panting and breathless.

"I love Van and Shane, but I have been *aching* to be alone with you." Mitch moves his hips and presses the straining in his jeans against mine as he says "aching."

I nod. Mitch grasps my hand and pulls me down the hall to my bedroom.

It seems we're getting right to it.

Mitch doesn't stop when we get in the bedroom. He keeps walking, tugging me to the bathroom.

"I think we both need a little relaxation, Posey. So, we are going to take a bath in that great big tub of yours."

I pull back on his hand. My bathroom is a mess. "Wait, I haven't used the tub in a few weeks."

"I know. I can tell by the piles of folded clothes in it."

I'm about to stop him when Mitch turns on the water. I peek in the tub and exhale. The clothes have been removed.

Mitch checks the water temperature and adds some lavender bath salts. He straightens and spins back to me. He runs his hands up and down my arms.

"Well, I think it's time for our first, of many to come, baths."

Mitch grasps the bottom of my T-shirt and pulls it over my head. He's undressing me for my bath. It's sweet and hot.

The T-shirt gone, Mitch trails kisses from behind my ear, down my neck and across my shoulder.

I regain the use of my limbs well enough to return the favor of removing Mitch's gray Henley.

I continue to rid him of the rest of his clothes, kissing the bared skin after each article is discarded. Mitch is successfully doing the same with mine until we're both down to our underwear when I notice the tub is getting really full.

"Mitch… the water!"

He quickly shuts off the tap, and with a slow scorching look over his shoulder, reaches down and pushes his boxer briefs down and off in a single movement. Mitch steps into the tub then extends his hand to me. He's erect. I can't help noticing.

I slip out of my panties and toss them behind me, attempting a carefree vibe. Really, I can't keep my eyes off him. His broad shoulders, rippled stomach and those *v*'s that direct my attention right to…

Mitch sits and positions me in front of him with my back to his front. The warmth of the water, the smell of lavender and his arms wrapped around me, slipping up and down my sides, occasionally moving high enough to graze my breasts, relaxes and excites.

One of Mitch's hands slides down to find my most sensitive spot. The other cups and massages my breast. I squirm and rotate my pelvis in response to his touch. The build comes on slowly but then notches up in waves. I pitch my head back and rest it on Mitch's shoulder. He turns and brings his lips crashing down on mine, kissing me into a fervor as my body tumbles into a spasming, mind-blowing orgasm. If he wasn't kissing me, I'm sure all the neighbors would have heard me moaning with joy.

Pushing myself away, I turn to face Mitch and lower myself onto him, splashing gallons of water out of the tub and onto the floor.

Mitch wraps his arms around my waist and seats me completely on him. I kiss him, and when he opens his mouth I suckle and swipe at his tongue. All while I ride and rock him until he grips my hips and thrusts into me while pulling me down.

His head falls back as he groans, "PO-sey!"

My core pulses around him as he lets go.

We've been in the bath so long getting dirty, we are now squeaky clean.

***

Cuddled in bed with Mitch, I'm far more at ease. We're spooning. Me in one of his concert T-shirts and him in a pair of soft joggers. Without underwear, I must note.

Mitch strokes some hair behind my ear, kisses the lobe and whispers, "Remember when I said I had a second question for you?"

"Yeah, that was a while ago. I thought maybe you'd already asked it."

"No, I've been waiting for the right moment."

"Oh." What could be so important he needed to wait for the right moment?

"You know the concert at the end of the semester?"

"Yes."

"Van is playing in it."

"He is?"

"Yes. Posey, can we go… together… as a couple?

I pause.

"What about…?" I sit up in bed.

Mitch sits up seconds after me, cups my shoulders and turns me to face him. "Don't finish that sentence. Who cares what anyone thinks? Anyone who matters is on board with this." He waves his hand in a circle between us. "Your kids, your parents, hell, even *my* parents and they haven't met you yet."

"What about the school moms? They talk. I know they do."

"The hell with them! They're just jealous because you are sexy as fuck. You could be, like, twenty-five years old."

"But I'm not."

"So, we should what? Wait? Until I'm twenty-six or twenty-eight or thirty? What would be appropriate, Posey? What would be right? What is the rule?"

"I don't know."

"No, we're not waiting, because I'm in love with you now. And I'm not wasting any time. If you've taught me one thing, it's don't waste time away from the one you love."

"You love me?"

"Yes."

I don't say it back. I change the subject. I have to be sure before I say those words. "Do you want kids?"

"I don't know."

"Because I'm thirty-eight and I don't know how much longer I have to do that."

"I'm not thinking about kids, but if I was I would only want them with you. And if we didn't, that would be OK, too, because the kids you have are already great. I could easily think of them as mine. Sort of already do."

"Are you sure?"

"Yes, Posey. This hesitancy isn't about Donovan, is it? This isn't about feeling wrong about... me... us?"

"No. No, no, no. I'm ashamed to say this but... this sounds so bad... but I don't feel him anymore. Actually, after he died, I never did. I missed him, but I never *felt* him. His spirit. People told me I'd feel him after he was gone, but I didn't. I never thought I'd seen him just around the corner or in another's face... until I met you."

"What?"

"I know it sounds nuts, but I saw things I loved and missed about him in you. I see all the things that made me fall in love with Donovan in you. Is that weird?"

"Little bit."

"Mostly, I love how much you love my kids and the way your eyes crinkle up when you smile. Like his did. Oh, I'm making this so weird." A single tear falls from my eye.

Mitch scoops me up in his arms. "It's OK, I'm OK with weird. If you can be OK with breaking the rules, even though they're really stupid rules."

"I know they are. I can be OK with that. Mitch, you know it's not just that, right. Not just that you remind me of him. Uhhhhh... how do I say this? It's the ways you're *not* him. It's more. I feel…" I take a deep breath and let it all spill out. "It's just *you*. I love the way you're honest and open with your feelings. How you let them show. To me. To everyone. I love how I am when I'm with you. I'm better—a better mom, a better me because of you." I finally wipe the tear away before it drips off my cheek.

Mitch's eyes are wet and he smiles crookedly. "Posey, baby, it's OK. I know. I know. I can tell how you feel about me. I'm just checking, but are you saying you… love me?"

"Yes, that's exactly what I'm saying. I love you, too."

"Finally! I thought you'd never say it back."

Chapter 15

Frantic, repeated knocks on the front door penetrate the quiet provided by my noise-cancelling headphones. I rip them off my head and the world becomes instantly loud and chaotic.

"Mom! Mom! Come out! Where are you? Shane got beat up on the bus!"

Stepping out of my studio, I look down the hall to the front of the house as Valley, Van and Mitch carrying Shane in his arms tumble into the foyer. My heart stops for a microbeat. They're followed by Valley's kids, one of them crying and the other loudly describing what happened.

"It was Rafe Walters."

Valley turns to Aiden. "Emily. I mean, Mrs. Walters's kid?"

Aiden nods.

"Figures," Valley comments, bitterly.

I rush to Shane perched on the kitchen counter where Mitch placed him. He's bawling, snot and blood both pouring from his nose, and his left eye starting to swell and color.

"Oh my God, sweetheart, Shaney, what happened? Is that who hurt you?"

Shane gulps and sniffles over and over. He can't catch his breath, but he nods yes. Van, Valley and her kids are all trying to explain at the same time. Mitch stands next to Shane, one arm around him supporting him and the other patting his knee. He quietly repeats "Shh, shh, shh" to Shane in rhythm to calm him down.

Shane's voice is small when he finally speaks. So soft, I can't hear him.

"Everyone! Shut up!" I roar from deep in my lungs. It does the trick. The room silences.

I take command. "Take another breath, baby. Take your time. Van, go get the first aid kit. Valley, find Emily Walters's phone number."

Shane takes three more deep breaths and finally speaks loud enough to be heard. "Rafe wa-wa-wa-was saying mean things."

"What mean things?"

"Mean things about you… He called you a cougar and a cradle robber. I said my mom is not a wild animal… or a baby stealer. I don't know what he meant, but his voice was mean."

"Oh, Shane."

I look up at Mitch.

His face is serious and his eyes glisten with tears. Then his face turn reds and he looks away. A muscle at his temple flexes. He stops patting Shane's knee and pulls his arm to his side, tensing and balling up his fist. "God dammit," he whispers.

Shane continues, "Then I told him to shut up and if my mom was a cougar, his mom was a baboon!"

Valley laughs, a little too loudly.

I shoot her a look.

"Then he called me a dummy and said my mom was dating the substitute music teacher, Mr. Morgan, who's only like nineteen. He said you were an old cougar and Mitch was fresh meat! That's when I went to hit him, but only barely got him on the arm and he, he…" Shane's voice breaks and he swallows down a sob. "He punched me across the nose and eye. So hard."

"I didn't see any of that," Van pipes in. "I was just getting home when I saw Shane all bloodied get off the bus. Valley was there and caught him. Mitch was just pulling into the driveway and saw us and ran over and got Shane."

I look up at Mitch. "You were subbing at Sunview Elementary?"

Mitch, who's been very quiet but still attentive to Shane replies, "Yes, they called early this morning with the job for a few days."

Shane smiles, even with his battered nose and puffy eye. "At the end of the day, when I was headed to the bus, I saw him in the hall. Mitch gave me a high five and said, 'See you tonight.' I told my friends, 'That's Mitch. My mom's boyfriend.'"

Valley whistles. "Whoa!"

Now, I freeze and look away. My little guy is so perceptive. He knew, even before we said anything.

"Rafe isn't very nice anyway. He's one of the big kids on

the bus. He just started teasing me for no reason," Shane says, finishing the story.

I question aloud, "Where would a kid that age hear that stuff?"

"Emily," Valley answers flatly. "She's a piece of work. I bet she saw you guys somewhere."

My heart pounds. The blood pulses in my ears. I am seething. But I don't want to show my anger in front of the kids.

Valley picks up on how completely enraged I am. "Posey, I'm gonna take the kids home. I'll text you that bitch's... Sorry, kids... I mean, Emily's number."

She hustles them out of the house but steps back in for a second. "Call me if you need anything. I mean it."

I send Van to his room, open the first aid kit and slowly and gently clean and dress Shane's injuries. I can't make eye contact with Mitch. I don't know exactly why I'm so agitated, but a voice inside me admonishes me, "Come on, you knew this was wrong, you knew it, but you went there anyway. Selfish. So selfish. And now look, your kid is hurt because of you."

"Posey!" Mitch reaches over to take the bandage package out of my hand and offer sympathy.

I flinch and step away. I hold a hand up when Mitch steps toward me. And then it happens. Vicious, thoughtless words shoot like poison darts from my mouth. "No, don't! Don't help! *THIS* is what I was talking about the other night. This. Us. It's wrong."

I love him, but I can't get used to having him around. I

can't risk my heart again. I can't risk my kids' hearts. I've been stupid to think I could do this.

"What are you saying, Posey?"

Irrationally I lash out at Mitch with the only thing about him that bothers me in the least. It's ridiculous and mean. "And why do you always knock on the door? Why don't you use the doorbell?"

"What?" Mitch looks puzzled, as if I'm speaking a foreign language.

"Mitch, a knock at a door. Think about it… in movies, stories, real life—"

"What? What does my knocking on the door have to do with—"

"Good things, good news is never preceded by a knock, Mitch. And you always knock. A knock always means bad news is coming."

"I just knock because sometimes doorbells don't work. What are you saying, Posey? Because I knock on the door instead of ringing the bell this happened to Shane?"

"Maybe. I don't know."

"Really? Are you saying I'm not a good thing? We're… not a good thing?"

I can't think straight and shake my head, not knowing what I mean.

Mitch cocks his head and pleads, "Posey?"

I'm bawling. I can't speak.

Shane is bawling, too. "Mooom, stop it!"

Mitch backs away, hands up, and spins on his heel and walks to the front door. He stops and says in a shaky voice,

"That's a pretty big reach, Posey. I love you. I've told you. And you love me. I'd never do anything to purposely hurt you or the boys." He sniffles loudly and swipes at his eyes.

Heaving sobs escape me. I need to speak, but can't. He's right. I'm reaching. I'm scared, and when I'm scared I retreat, run away, play myself out. I get away before I get hurt. What the hell am I doing?

"I'll just leave," he says and is out the door.

I take a few worthless steps toward the door as it closes behind him.

Van appears next to me. "Mom! Mom, stop him! You can't let him leave. You can't let him go." He heard all of the ruckus from the hallway.

But I do. I watch Mitch walk away and I just stand there.

The three of us, Shane, Van and I, say nothing to each other. Van runs to his room and slams the door. Shane's crying ramps up.

I wipe my tears, finish cleaning up Shane's face and call the school and the bus company, while waiting for the Walters's number from Valley. I've set up a meeting first thing tomorrow morning with the principal and the bus company manager. They're calling Rafe Walters's parents.

Shane has fallen asleep on the couch in the family room, an ice pack on his face and medicated with a whopping dose of ibuprofen.

I sit in my chair and watch my youngest son breath in and out softly. He's finally calm and comfortable. My baby was hurt because he was defending me. Defending my relationship with Mitch. A ten-year-old shouldn't have to do that.

Checking my phone, there's no text from Valley. Or Mitch. Why would Mitch text me? I was horrible to him. I've hurt Mitch by attacking him and pushing him away.

I text them both, begging them to call or text me. I don't know what I'm doing.

Eventually, I pick up Shane and carry him to bed. Kissing him on the forehead before I leave the room. I peek in on Van. He's fallen asleep in his clothes on top of his bed. I grab a blanket off a chair in his room and place it over him. I don't kiss him for fear of waking him up, but I do kiss two of my fingers and then place them on his cheek lightly. He rolls away from me to his side. I back out of the room and shut off his light.

The doorbell rings once, just as I'm closing Van's door.

Looking down the hall, I see a familiar form through the frosted window of the front door.

Mitch.

Chapter 16

I can't get to the front door fast enough. Opening it, I apologize immediately. "Mitch, I'm sorry. I'm so, so sorry. I don't know what made me act like that."

Mitch smiles a thin line of a smile. His eyes are red. "I rang the doorbell." He points at the bell.

I don't care, I'm just so happy he came back.

I don't even invite him in, I just start blabbing. "You don't have to do that. I'm a complete bitch. You can knock. In fact, I insist you knock. I need to learn that a knock on the door is just that. Someone coming to see me. A good thing. In your case, a wonderful thing. The best thing to happen to me in a long time. Or maybe you should just walk in. There's no need for you to knock ever again to come into this house."

His smile broadens. "I'll do whatever makes you happy, babe. I just don't want what happened this afternoon to ever happen again. If I'm doing something that upsets you, you have to tell me, OK?"

"OK. Mitch, I was wrong."

"Yes, you were."

I laugh, a little honest laugh. "None of this is your fault. Shane didn't get hurt because you knocked on the door. He didn't get hurt because we're together—"

"He got hurt," he interrupts, "because his parents are loudmouthed idiots who don't know kids pick up on things. Meanness is learned at home. Bullying is learned at home."

I rush to him and he enfolds me in his arms. He kisses my forehead and then tips my tear-stained, puffy, exhausted face up and kisses me so softly, so full of care.

"I thought you might not come back," I croak, my voice rough from crying.

"Of course I came back. I just needed a minute. I needed to think about a few things. I'm here for you, Posey. For you and the boys. I love you. I love those boys."

"Oh my God, I love you. How did we get so lucky to have you in our lives?"

"And Pose, I'm going with you to meet with the school and Rafe Walters's parents tomorrow."

"How did you know about that?"

"I just know."

"O-OK."

Mitch cocks his head and smirks, "Can we go inside now?"

I realize we are still lingering in the open doorway. I step back and tug him into the house by his shirt.

Mitch slides his hand down my arm and threads his fingers between mine. He brings my hand up to his lips and kisses my knuckles one by one.

"You look exhausted and I know I am. Let's go to bed."

We walk to my bedroom, hand in hand. Halfway there, I rest my head on his shoulder. I'm more tired than I realized.

Mitch and I quietly change into our nightclothes quietly. We slide under the covers. Mitch spoons with me.

"Good night, my Posey. I'm right here. I'm never leaving again." The feel of his lips delivering sweet, tiny kisses on my neck and the low timbre of his voice soothe me. I sigh with relief and contentment and drift off.

***

Knock! Knock! Knock!

I sit straight up in bed.

Knock! Knock! Knock!

What now? I rub my eyes and twist to plant my feet on the floor.

Knock! Knock! Knock!

I don't turn on any lights as I make my way down the hall. There's just enough light to find the way with the light coming in the windows from the streetlights and the few night-lights I keep in case the boys wake up.

Knock! Knock! Knock!

Whoever is at the door is going to wake everyone up. I open the front door a crack. There's someone backed away from the door, but there's a bright, white light behind them so I can only see the outline of his body.

"Posey," a deep, dreamy, so-familiar-to-me voice says.

"Donnie?" But how can that be? I step forward, shielding

my eyes against the light to see him more clearly.

He moves, as if on a conveyor belt or flying just above the ground, and suddenly, the face I've loved for so long is right in front of me. But different than I remember. Smoother, shinier, completely free of pain or anxiety.

"Posey, you are going to be OK."

"But, how are you here?"

He doesn't answer my question but continues, "I'm sorry I left you. I didn't want to."

I reach out for Donnie, but he's just far enough away that I can't touch him.

He smiles, the smile where his eyes crinkle, but they don't crinkle as much now. He looks almost… angelic. "I want to touch you, too, sweetheart, but I can't. Posey, I want you to know something. You deserve to have someone who loves you as much as I did. I think you've found him."

Mitch!

Donnie kisses his fingers and blows me a kiss. "I just want you to be happy, Posey. I will always love you. Tomorrow starts a whole new life."

I can't stand it. I want to hold him. I walk forward with my arms out, but instead of waiting for my embrace, Donnie turns, floats down the sidewalk and fades, dissolving before my eyes and washing away like a beautiful chalk drawing in the rain.

"Don't go," I plead, my voice thin and tight. "Donnie!" I'm losing him again and letting him go all at once.

My heart squeezes. I close my eyes tight and consciously acknowledge that I must be dreaming. This can't be happening.

When I open my eyes, I'm no longer standing at the front door. I'm in my bed, lying next to Mitch. Crying. Gentle tears. Happy Tears. I *was* dreaming. The best dream.

I turn over in bed to face him. "Mitch, Mitch, wake up!"

Yawning and blinking awake, Mitch reaches out and pulls me close. "What's wrong, Pose. Baby? Why are you crying?"

"I saw him. Donnie. In a dream." I tell Mitch about my dream, every second of it. "Mitch, it's all going to be OK. I finally felt Donnie and he wants me to move on."

"Oh, my Posey." My new love holds me close, kisses all my tears away and breathes in rhythm with me.

"Mitch, I didn't think I could ever feel… feel like this again. Feel completely free to love anyone but Donnie. But us?" I pull back so I can look into Mitch's green eyes. "This is real, isn't it?"

"Yes, it's absolutely real."

Even though we are both physically and emotionally drained, Mitch makes love to me. Slow, deliberate love. Full of a connection that's so much more than physical.

Chapter 17

Sitting in my car in my driveway Wednesday night after work, I process the last twenty-four hours. It was a very long emotional night that was followed by a very long day.

I finally get out after staying in my car long enough to hear Tom Petty's "Breakdown" all the way through. I think about the words of the song as I exit the car.

Valley barrels across the street just as I reach my door, still caught up in my thoughts.

She's out of breath and at my side in no time. "So, Mitch, he really went with you to the meeting with Emily and Gary Walters?"

I wave her into the house. "Come. Come in. And yes. How did you know about that?"

"Mitch texted me after he went over to the Walters's last night." Valley explains as if I already know this.

I stop just inside the doorway, completely at a loss. "He went over to the Walters's house? Last night?"

Valley grimaces with her teeth together, sucking in air through them. "Shiiiit! I wasn't supposed to tell you that."

I direct us to the dining room table, throwing all my stuff, my purse and laptop case on top of it, and motion to Valley to sit.

"Well, you're already wet, so you might as well go swimming. Spill. What happened last night that I don't know?"

Valley shakes her head. "Man, he's going to kill me."

"Valley!" I admonish.

"So, Mitch came over to my house last night, and he was fucking bawling like a baby. Said you were so mad at him. That you thought Shane got hurt because of him."

I correct her. "Not him, us. I just said the meanest, stupidest things."

"Well, it gutted him."

A sob catches in my throat. I'll be making all that up to him for quite a while.

"He knew you were just scared and upset. He knew you'd calm down, but he didn't know what to do."

"Jesus, I'm a bitch."

"No, you're a mom and someone who's been hurt."

The sob escapes as a squeaky gulp.

"Anyway," Valley continues, "Mitch wanted to do something to make it better. He got the Walters's phone number and address from me. That's why I didn't share it with you. I thought he was giving it to you, but he didn't. He left my house and I thought he was coming back here."

"He did."

"Yes, but not before paying a visit to the Walters family."

"What?"

"Yeah, he left my house and went over there. I don't know what he said to Emily and Gary, but he seemed satisfied when he texted me back. He said you had a meeting with them today and he was going."

It strikes me that Mitch must have gotten to the Walters's just after the school called to inform them of the meeting. "Come to think of it, Emily was super apologetic and Gary just kept his head down and his sunglasses on the whole time. I couldn't tell if he was sorry or being an asshole. I wonder what he said to them."

Valley laughs. "Gary was wearing sunglasses because Mitch punched him in the fucking eye."

"No! Really?"

"Yeah, he didn't want you or Shane to know, but he wanted Gary to feel some of the pain Shane did. Mitch felt bad about it because he knew you'd think violence was *not* the answer. He just couldn't help himself."

I love Mitch even more. In theory, I don't approve of what he did, but personally, I feel so loved and protected. That my boys are loved and protected.

"Yes, Mitch was at the meeting. He was amazing. He didn't say anything. He just stood by my side and agreed with me. Supported me."

Valley reaches over and pats my hand. "Looks like you guys are back on track. Listen to me. Hold onto this guy. He loves the fuck out of you. You won't find another one like him."

"But he's so young."

"So what? Good for you."

"What if I'm not enough for him? Not young enough, pretty enough? I'll look older sooner than he will. And what if he needs more? More kids?"

Valley shakes her head. "Posey, stop worrying. About what others think. About how you look. You look fucking awesome and will for years. You're more than enough for him. I can tell by the way he talks about you. Trust Mitch. I have a feeling he's never leaving your side ever again."

Chapter 18

Mitch and Van took their guitars and mini amps and left Shane and me in the audience. It's the night of the all-district school concert. Van and some of the other kids Mitch teaches privately have been invited to play a couple of numbers after the school bands. This is due to all of Mitch's subbing and networking with the music teachers. He even told me he interviewed for a full-time job at Sunview Middle School.

I sit patiently through one number after another until, at last, the curtains open to Van. Up on the stage, alone, his guitar in front of him. A single spotlight on him.

"This song is for the four people who always have my back. You know who you are." He points up to the sky for Donovan, out to the audience for me and Shane and then looks offstage to his right. I may be the only one who knows it, but I know he's looking at Mitch.

Van sings the first few lines of "Our House," the Crosby, Stills and Nash song, not the one by Madness. I never knew his voice was so good. How did I not hear him practice this?

I can tell he means every word. When he gets to the line about how life used to be so hard, but now everything is easy because of you, I know he means it for Mitch.

The "aws" in the crowd are audible. I can hear several moms near me sniffling. I catch a glimpse of Emily Walters. Even she has tears in her eyes. I lift my chin. She reciprocates. We've reached a silent agreement, it seems. She'll be a kinder person and encourage her kid to do the same. I'll keep my boyfriend from pummeling her husband. Actually, I think there will be no need now that Mitch is Rafe's guitar teacher, too. Only he could turn a confrontation into a new opportunity.

Mitch and four of his other guitar students come out and join Van on the chorus of the song.

"La, la, la la la, la!" the audience sings along. Mitch stands next to Van and shares the microphone.

As the song comes to an end, another guitar comes through, louder over all the others. The tune morphs and I recognize the first few chords. This song isn't out in the world yet. It's a secret. The one I've been listening to on repeat for months.

"Ladies and gentlemen, as a special surprise, we have for you… Sid Cooper from #coolNerd," Mitch announces over all the music.

The audience is on their feet the moment he steps on the stage.

And there he is, the man I've been most focused on lately, other than Mitch. Sid Cooper, here, in the Sunview Middle School Auditorium. Redheaded, nerdy, tattooed and playing the guitar like an angel plays a harp. What a surprise for the school district, but really for me.

I look down at Shane. He's smiling but unfazed. He looks up at me and winks.

I mouth, "Did you know?"

Shane nods vigorously.

"Sneaky. All of you."

"How did this happen?"

"Mom, Mitch is really good friends with Sid. They went to school together in Illinois."

There are still things I don't know about Mitch that, evidently, my kids do. This must be the friend he was talking about. The one who was trying to get him to go on the road.

Mitch moves aside to give Sid the place in front of the microphone.

"Hello, everyone! I'm Sid. My friend Mitch here gave me a call and said there was a big concert here at Sunview. I hope you don't mind me crashing."

The crowd whistles and cheers amid those yelling, "No!" and "We don't mind!"

"I thought I'd sing you my newest song. It's not even on the radio yet, but coming out soon. I wrote it for my sister and brother-in-law, Minnie and Snack, but tonight it goes out to another couple. Posey and Mitch, this one's for you."

My mouth drops open. Sid Cooper just outed my relationship to the entire school community. Basically, the entire town. I feel every single set of eyes on me. I look at Mitch grinning at me like a maniac. He stops playing long enough to make a heart over his heart with two hands and then points at me. It's one of those things, one of the ways Mitch shows he loves me. I would have thought it was completely dorky until I fell for him. Now I know, it's just Mitch.

"So, I'm going to play 'You Are My New Home' from my album coming out real soon. By the way, thank you, Posey, for the great work on the cover art."

Shane hugs my legs. Van beams from his spot onstage right next to Sid.

I'm congratulated and hugged and high-fived from all sides by parents and kids.

I've spent a lot of time looking for signs from Donovan since he died. I'd never felt his presence until the dream, and I don't really believe in signs. This night, right now, feels like a sign.

When I look up to the stage again, Mitch is not there. He's walking down to me in the audience. I wiggle out of the row to get to him, meeting him halfway.

"I love you."

"I love you."

The words are in stereo as we both, very publicly, profess our feelings and announce our relationship status.

More "aws." Even one from Sid onstage.

Mitch kisses me, picks me up and spins me around. He stops and slowly places me on the ground. In this moment, we are all alone. Sid, Van, Shane, everyone in the audience, everyone in the world are gone. It's just him. Just me.

"Posey, I know this is all new. All I need in this world to be happy is you, and wherever you want this to go, that's what I want, too. Tell me you feel the same. Because if you say you do, that you'll be with me officially, and well… then tomorrow starts a whole new life."

Tomorrow starts a whole new life. The last words Donovan said to me.

I don't know if I want marriage or more kids. Right now, I just want Mitch.

"Yes, we're official."

Mitch says "Yes!" loudly and throws his arms out to his sides before placing his forehead against mine.

"Breathe, Posey. Breathe out and I promise I'll always be here to breathe you in."

I let go of the breath I didn't know I was holding.

Maybe I've been holding it for three years.

And I breathe in my new life.

THE END

About the Author

Emme Burton is the author of the award-winning, Top 50 Rom-Com, SNACK; the Better Than Series: Better Than Me, Fix It For Us, and Still Into You; and AwKwaRD, Victoria. She was a contributing author to the bestselling anthologies,  Hook & Ladder 69 and Bleed Blue 69. She lives in St. Louis, Missouri with her amazing husband and sons. Emme has never, ever been lost in a mall either as a child or an adult. Her mother, and now her family, have always known where to find her. At the bookstore.

Like Emme's Facebook Page: Author Emme Burton
Follow her on Twitter: @EmmeBurton
Add her books to your TBR on GoodReads.
Emme's Website: www.emmeburton.com

Other Books in the Juniper Court Series

You'll also find teasers, deleted scenes, and more on the website: www.junipercourtseries.com

More Books by Emme Burton:

Better Than Me (Book 1, Better Than Series)
Fix It For Us (Book 2, Better Than Series)
Still Into You (Book 3, Better Than Series)
Snack
AwKwaRd, Victoria
Hook & Ladder 69, 18 Authors, 1 Hot Firehouse (An Anthology)
Bleed Blue 69, 25 Authors, 1 Hot Precinct (An Anthology)

Inside info: The Knock features Donovan and Posey Garrett
from The Better Than Series and Sid Cooper from Snack.